THE WOLF'S BITE

ISBN-13: 978-1-63696-095-1
ISBN-10: 1-63696-095-2

Cover design by: Damonza
Printed in the United States of America

DAVID ARCHER

THE WOLF'S BITE

A
NOAH WOLF
THRILLER

R

RIGHT HOUSE

Fate whispers to the wolf; "you cannot withstand the storm." The wolf whispers back, "I am the storm."

ONE

Noah's phone vibrated in his pocket, and he took it out to read the text message that had just come in.

My office 13:00.

He looked up at Sarah and Neil, who were sitting across his kitchen table from him. They had been eating lunch, but their phones had gone off at the same time as his, and he knew they were reading the same message.

"I guess the Dragon Lady thinks it's time to get us back in the saddle," Neil said.

Sarah nodded. "I've kinda been expecting it," she said. "It's been a month. I'm surprised they gave us that long."

Neil looked up at Noah. "Don't suppose they gave you any heads up on what's happening, did they?"

"No," Noah said. "I'm sure this has to do with filling the gap in our team. With Moose gone, we need a new backup man. I would imagine we're going to meet him today."

Neil and Sarah looked at one another but didn't say anything. They had both felt the incredible impact of Moose's loss, but they had finally stopped breaking into tears each time they thought of him. Moose Conway had been more than just a part of their team; he had been like a brother to each of them, and had given his life in an effort to save theirs. Their last mission, to ferret out the people behind a little-known but powerful terrorist organization, had gone sour and they had been forced to go after one of the most deadly assassins the world had ever known. When it came down to a firefight, that assassin had drawn a bead on Neil, but Moose had drawn his fire and taken the bullet. His heroism had cost him his life.

Noah Wolf, their team leader, had fired the shots that ended that assassin's career, along with his life. Noah was an assassin, himself, the shining star of the American organization known simply as E & E. He had been recruited after a short but illustrious military career, specifically because he suffered from something known as atypical blunted affect disorder, a rare condition that leaves its victims without emotions—or conscience—of any kind. Noah had not been afflicted with the ravaging grief that Sarah and Neil had known, but he still felt the vacancy that Moose's death had left in his life. There was something wrong, with Moose gone, something that simply would never be right again in Noah's world.

Unfortunately, the work that they did was dangerous. As an assassin, it was often up to Noah to eliminate dangerous or evil persons from the world, just the way any soldier might have to eliminate an enemy. There were always risks in any kind of war, and Moose was not the first to die in the service of E & E, nor would he be the last. Noah had come to the conclusion that the Grim Reaper knew each of their names, and probably had them written on some future to-do list.

"Man," Neil said, "I hope whoever we get isn't an asshole. Moose is gonna be a tough act to follow."

"It's almost a quarter after twelve," Sarah said. "We should probably get on the way, if we're going to get there on time."

She put away the bread and cold cuts they had used for making sandwiches while Noah cleared their plates and put them in the dishwasher. Neil walked out ahead of them and managed to twist his long, lanky frame into the back seat of Sarah's Camaro when they joined him. Noah slid into the front passenger seat as Sarah got behind the wheel, and they headed into Kirtland.

Sarah had to push the car a bit to make it on time, but they stepped out of the elevator at two minutes before one. Getting to Allison's office took only a minute, so they were actually slightly early when her secretary waved them in.

Don Jefferson, Allison's right-hand man, was already sitting on one of the big leather sofas in her office. Allison was in the wingback chair she used when she was holding an informal meeting, so Noah and the others settled onto the sofa across from the one Jefferson occupied.

Allison Peterson was the director of E & E. She answered only to the President of the United States, and her approval was required before any assassination could be ordered by American operatives. In most cases, any assassination she sanctioned would be carried out by one of the teams that worked for her.

"I'm assuming you've all had time to cope with the loss of Mr. Conway," Allison said without preamble. "We understand how devastating such a loss can be to a team, but it's also necessary to get you past it and back into action as soon as possible. We have to replace him today, and your new teammate will be here in just a few minutes."

"Because you're our very best team," Jefferson said, "we're giving you the best man we have available. His

3

name is Marco Turin, and I'm fairly sure you've all met him before."

Noah nodded. "I have," he said. "He showed me around my first day here, but you know that. He struck me then as a pretty good guy."

"He's an asshole," Neil said with a disappointed sigh. "When I was in PT, he was always picking on me about how tall I am."

Sarah grinned at him. "That's because most people aren't tall enough to bang their heads on a doorway." She turned to Jefferson. "I've met him a couple of times, just around town. He seems okay."

Allison rolled her eyes. "Good, that's two out of three of you he won't have to win over. Listen, kids, it's very rough on anyone who has to step in when a team member is lost. Don't be too hard on him, okay?"

There was a tap on the door, and it opened to reveal Marco. He grinned when he saw Noah and stepped into the room, taking a seat beside Jefferson.

Marco was a dark-haired, stocky and muscular man of about five foot ten. His hair was a little long and parted in the middle, and he wore a short and obviously un-trimmed beard. He sat quietly for a few seconds, simply allowing the team to look him over. When he finally spoke, it was softly, and with an accent that sounded like the Deep South.

"When they told me I was gonna be joining your team," he said, "I remembered Noah and I talked about that possibility when we first met. I know you had a good run with Moose, and I can tell you that I had nothing but the greatest respect for him. I know I can never replace him, but I promise you I'll do my best at whatever you need me to do."

Noah leaned forward and extended a hand to him. "I'm sure you will," he said. "None of us expect you to become Moose, so just be yourself. That's all we ask."

Neil shook hands with Marco, and then Sarah followed suit. "Just don't start with the tall jokes, okay?" Neil asked. "Let's leave that behind us."

Marco grinned. "No problem," he said. "I never make jokes about a man I always look up to."

Neil groaned, but Sarah chuckled. "We're all just here to do our jobs," she said. "You'll be fine, I'm sure."

Allison smiled at them all. "Marco has been our utility man, filling in wherever he was needed up until now. This will be his first permanent assignment to a team, but there was literally no one better that we could give you." She leaned forward and put her elbows on her knees, her hands clasped together. "Noah, I want you guys to spend the next few days getting used to each other, because there's a mission waiting for you. I won't go into the specifics right now, but I need your team ready to start mission-specific training next Monday morning."

Jefferson cleared his throat. "I'd suggest you spend your time recreationally until then," he said. "Try to spot any personality differences that could interfere and overcome them, because there won't be time for it once your training begins. The new mission will be critical, but it's also going to be different from what you've done up till now. We need to know you guys can work together properly."

"That's it for the moment," Allison said. "You kids get out of here and go have some fun. We'll all meet again oh eight hundred Monday morning, in the briefing room."

Noah stood and the others all rose immediately after. "Okay," he said. "Let's go have a beer."

"Sounds good," Marco said. He and the others followed

Noah out the door, and they rode down the elevator together. "Hey, Stretch, why don't you ride with me?" He pointed at the Mustang that was parked two spaces over from Sarah's Camaro.

Neil glared at him. "Do not call me that," he said menacingly. "Remember that I can spit onto your head without you even noticing, okay?"

Marco laughed. "Okay, okay, I just had to get one more out of my system. I promise I won't do it again, good enough?"

Neil's narrowed eyes bore into him for a moment, but then he nodded. "Okay, fine," he said. He followed Marco to the Mustang and slid the passenger seat all the way back before he got in.

Noah and Sarah got into the Camaro and backed out, and she led the way out of the garage. "Where to?" she asked Noah.

"Let's go on out to the Sagebrush," Noah said, naming their favorite restaurant and bar. "A beer actually does sound pretty good about now."

Sarah nodded and pointed the car in that direction. From town, it took them almost 30 minutes to get to the saloon, and she was just mischievous enough to force Marco to break the speed limits to keep up with her. When they pulled into the parking lot, Noah noticed that both Marco and Neil were grinning when they got out of the car.

They walked into the restaurant and were greeted by Don Jefferson's daughter, Elaine. Elaine had been Moose's girlfriend, and the smile she gave them had a hint of sadness in it. "Hey, Guys," she said. She looked Marco over. "This the new guy?"

"Yep," Sarah said. "Elaine, this is Marco. Marco, this is

Elaine Jefferson."

Marco and Elaine nodded at one another. "We've met before," Elaine said. "You've got a rough job ahead of you, Marco. Filling Moose's shoes isn't going to be easy."

"I'm not even gonna try," Marco said. "We all know he was the best at what he did, so I'm just going to try to do my job the best I can."

Elaine looked into his eyes for a moment, then nodded once. "That's good," she said. "Moose and I were pretty close, but I love the rest of these guys, too. You better take care of them for me, whenever you're out on the job."

Marco grinned and winked. "That's my plan," he said.

"Good," she said. "Come on, guys, I've got a table right over here."

Elaine led them to a table that was situated some distance away from the few other customers in the restaurant, then brought them each the beer they had ordered. Neil, who was actually still a few months shy of being old enough to drink legally, knew that she wouldn't bother to card him.

The table had five chairs. Noah took one, with his back to the wall, with Sarah sitting beside him on his left and Neil on the opposite side of her. Marco had taken the chair on Noah's right, and now he nodded at the fifth chair.

"Are we expecting someone else?"

"No," Noah said. "That's Moose's chair. It's sort of a tradition we developed after we lost him."

"Yeah," Neil said. "He's always with us, so we always keep a chair open for him."

Marco nodded. "I get it," he said. "Look, y'all, it's like I told Elaine. I'm not out to replace him, I've been around the outfit enough to know that that's impossible. You guys all had something going, something that let you work together in one of the worst possible jobs you could ever have. Believe me when I say I'm fully aware that I may never find that same closeness. I've been a utility man for the last two years, filling in wherever they needed me. Don't worry about making me feel like the odd man out, I'm used to it. Just know that I'll do my absolute best at whatever y'all need me to do."

Noah cocked his head and looked at Marco quizzically. "No problem there," he said. "I'm just wondering, though, where did you get that Southern drawl? I don't remember you sounding like that back when we met."

Marco laughed. "Back then I was doing all I could not to let it show," he said. "Lately, I just got to the point I don't worry about it. It comes from my upbringing. I grew up down in Florida, in a small town near the Georgia line."

"Good," Neil said. "Next time you make wise cracks about how tall I am, I'll remind you that you're just a cracker."

The four of them made small talk through a couple of beers apiece, then Noah suggested they all head back to his place. They settled their tabs with Elaine, leaving the generous tip they always did, and Noah noticed that Neil automatically went to the passenger door of Marco's car.

It looked like Marco might just fit in.

TWO

"This is likely to be one of the toughest missions we'll ever give you," Allison said during their briefing on the following Monday. "It is not, and I repeat not, an assassination. This time you get to experience the other E, eradication. The goal this time is to make the target disappear and seem to be dead, while we move them into an entirely new life."

"That's only one of the differences," Jefferson said, sitting beside her at the conference table. "Another one is that it won't be Noah on point position, this time. The target is a young woman who is currently held in a women's prison in Thailand. Sarah, you'll be going into the prison yourself to make contact. Noah and the others will be planning and arranging your escape, so your job is to get this girl to come with you."

Sarah's eyes had gone suddenly wide. "I have to go to prison?"

"Yes," Allison said. "You'll be arrested for possession of methamphetamine, the most common charge in Thailand. As a result, you'll be quickly sentenced to a term of years in the prison known as the 'Bangkok Hilton.' A part of it is designated as a women's prison, and that's where you'll find your target." He pushed a button on a remote he held in his hand, and the image of a pretty young woman with long brown hair appeared on the screen behind him. "That's her. Her name is Sharon Ingersoll, and she's been sentenced to five years for possession and sale of *yaba*, or meth."

"Wait," Neil said, "we're going into a prison to rescue a drug dealer?"

"Actually, no," Allison said. "Miss Ingersoll was innocent. She was simply visiting Thailand on vacation, and was sharing a room with another American girl that she met after she arrived. That girl had purchased the drugs for her own use, but because it was more than what the government there recognizes as a recreational amount and they were both in the room at the time, both of them were charged. Thailand doesn't provide any kind of quality in defense attorneys and she wasn't given a chance to secure her own, so they were railroaded through a rapid trial, convicted and sentenced in less than a week."

"Okay, but still," Neil went on. "If she was innocent, isn't there something our embassy could do? Why does it have to involve us?"

"As it happens," Jefferson took over, "Miss Ingersoll is considered a rising star in the field of particle beam technology. She's been working with DARPA for the last two years, and the research team she's part of insists they can't continue without her. The work she does concerns mostly weapons and energy transmission and is classified Most Secret, so normal diplomatic channels that require tons of background information could run the risk of exposing her. If any of our enemies were to learn about her current situation, she'd be at risk of abduction or termination, so the Joint Chiefs want us to move on this as soon as possible. Since she has no family, and very few friends outside of those she works with, a complete change of identity seems to be the ideal solution."

Sarah swallowed hard. "Okay," she said. "And how do we get her out?"

"That's going to be the tricky part," Jefferson said. "We considered trying to bribe the guards, but that runs the risk of discovery that could make the mission even more difficult. The most likely chance of success is going to come down to a stealth incursion. Noah, Neil and Marco are going to have to break into the prison, locate you and the target, and then get you both out."

"Earth to Jefferson," Neil said. "You're including me in this insanity? You do remember that I'm the clumsy one, right?"

Jefferson grinned at him. "Of course," he said. "But don't worry, Neil, we've got you covered. Ms. Ingersoll was arrested almost two months ago, so we've had some time to work on the problem. We've had a detailed mockup of the prison constructed out in the training areas, and filled it with more than a hundred actors who have been briefed on how the staff and prisoners would act. It's accurate even down to the colors of the walls, so you'll be able to practice every move dozens of times before you actually get on the plane to Thailand. You've got a week; I'm sure you can get it down to a science in that time, can't you?"

Neil rolled his eyes and sank into his seat. Noah leaned forward slightly.

"You said a stealth incursion," he said. "What about weapons?"

"Special and silent," Jefferson replied. "While there aren't many escapes from the Bangkok Hilton, it has happened in the past. Usually, it involves help from someone on the inside, but this one is going to be different. You'll have some special weapons for this mission, because you've got to make every effort not to leave any corpses behind you, this time. Live guards who were stunned or don't know what happened will probably be punished for dereliction of duty, but dead guards would be grounds for a massive investigation. The last thing we need is for anyone to associate the escape of a pair of American girls with potential agencies of the US government."

"And that's exactly what they would think," Allison added. "The diplomatic nightmare that would ensue would make the fallout over Benghazi look like a picnic. I'm not telling you not to take whatever steps are necessary to accomplish the mission, Noah, I'm just asking you to be very, very careful. I told R&D to work up some nonlethal weapons for you. Hopefully, that will avoid leaving any bodies in your wake."

"Okay," Noah said. "Mr. Jefferson, you said there is a mockup of the prison for us to practice in?"

"Yep, a duplicate of the women's section. The entire prison is pretty large, but the women are housed in one small part of it. That section is up against what amounts to the eastern walls of the prison, so we made a mockup of about a fifth of the whole structure. It's laid out exactly like the real thing, so you'll be able to get familiar with every twist and turn you might have to make when you go in."

"Now," Allison interrupted, "the trickiest part will be after you get them out. You have to stage the escape in such a way that it leaves a trail, and some of our operatives in Bangkok will provide you with a corpse that has been modified to look a lot like Ms. Ingersoll, even down to the fingerprints. The body is of a young woman who has been declared brain-dead after a drug overdose but is currently being kept alive on the physical level. A portable life support unit will keep it breathing until it's time for Ms. Ingersoll to become officially dead, and then, Noah, you will fire the shot that will become her official cause of death. Once they have the body, the Thai authorities will be more than happy to close the case on her. Sarah, of course, will simply disappear with you. She'll become one of the legends of people who escaped the Bangkok Hilton."

"That's a relief," Sarah said. "For a minute there, I was afraid I was going to have to get caught with the corpse in order to make it all convincing."

"Oh, no," Allison said with a grin. "You're not getting away that easily, young lady. We still need you."

"I'm glad to hear it," Sarah said, smiling.

Allison turned to Noah. "Noah, despite your lack of normal emotions, I know that you've gone to extreme lengths to rescue Sarah in the past. I have to ask this question, even though I don't want to. Is this situation we are putting her in going to create a problem?"

"No, Ma'am," Noah said without hesitation. "I understand the necessity, and rescuing her seems to be part of my regular job description, anyway. The mission comes first."

"Hey!" Sarah said, but she was grinning.

"Don't get your panties in a bunch," Neil said. "We all know good and well that Noah won't let anything bad happen to you."

Marco chuckled. "Heck, yeah, even I can tell that."

Allison smiled, but her eyes were boring into Noah. "It is necessary, and there isn't another team I could trust with this mission. I'm counting on you, Camelot."

"Yes, Ma'am," Noah said. "How soon can we begin training?"

"Today. I want you to make a stop out to see Wally, then report to the training center. The gate will know where to send you, and someone will be there to give you a tour. Start working up your mission plans as soon as possible, Noah, because DARPA wants this girl back within the next three weeks. That gives you one week training, one week to get into position and one to pull it all off. If anyone can do it, I know that Team Camelot can."

The team rose, and Neil grabbed a couple of extra doughnuts on his way out of the briefing room. They had ridden to the briefing in his Hummer, so they climbed back into it in the parking garage and headed out to see Wally at the R&D section.

THREE

Wally Lawson missed out on becoming a mad scientist only because he just didn't have enough evil in his heart. Had that not been the case, he might well have been the type of genius who could invent orbital death rays and use them to blackmail every nation on the earth to submit to his domination.

Still, Wally's need to devise creative methods of dealing death and destruction seemed to be inherent in him, and so he had submitted patent applications for several items that would have made James Bond sit up and take notice, all before the age of seventeen. Someone in the patent office had enough intelligence to realize just what the devices were capable of, and referred them to the FBI, who then passed them on to the CIA. A week later, Wally was paid a visit by three people claiming to represent a major defense contractor. Since he had already graduated high school two years earlier and dropped out of college simply because it was boring, he happily accepted the lucrative income that came with the job they offered him in their research department.

Wally Lawson was a genius. Despite a massive charade, it took him less than three days to figure out who he was really working for. That didn't bother him, so he was running the entire department by the time he was twenty-two. He'd held that position for more than twelve years.

Allison had learned about Wally while she herself worked for the CIA, so when the president tasked her with creating E & E, she had demanded the right to take him along. He'd been with the agency for three years and seemed to be happier than ever. He had also brought along some of the talent he had been developing for the company, and Allison's recruiting had brought him several more. The R&D center covered almost 30 acres and employed more than sixty people with degrees ranging from engineering to physics and even quantum mechanics. Many of their creations could do things that would've still been thought impossible with publicly known technology, but they remained highly classified.

The security guards, who all knew Noah and the others by sight—even Marco had been there numerous times—nevertheless spent more than a minute carefully examining their identification and confirming their identities with retinal scans. Once they were satisfied they were not dealing with impostors, they opened the inner door and allowed the team to enter.

"Camelot!" Wally shouted as he walked quickly up the hall toward them. He stopped in front of Noah and extended a hand, and the two men shook. "They called ahead and told me you were coming. I got a quick briefing on your mission last month, so I've had my people working round-the-clock to come up with ways to help you out. Ready to see what they've got for you?"

"Yes," Noah said. "I hope they're giving us something good. Sarah's going to be dangerously exposed on this mission, and I don't want anything to happen to her. She's been through enough already."

"Well, yeah," Wally said. "Don't you worry, we'll keep her as safe as we possibly can." He stopped and looked at Marco, then turned his eyes back to Noah. His normally jovial face turned solemn. "I was really sad to hear about Moose," he said. "He was one of the best."

"Yes, but he was also a soldier. We all know the risks of our job, and Moose gave his life to protect Sarah and Neil, and even me. I suspect his only regret would be missing out on the next mission."

"Amen," Neil said. "That was Moose."

Wally nodded, and then the smile spread over his face again. "I see they gave you Marco," he said. "He's pretty good, think he can keep up with you guys?"

Noah glanced at Marco. "He's going to have to. We're being tossed right into the fray, but I think he knows what he's doing. We'll all do the jobs we have to do, and do them the best we can."

"Okay, then, let's go see what we've got. I put Nancy and Mickey in charge of this project, they're right down this hall." He turned and started walking even before he finished. Noah and his team followed along.

They came to a green door and Wally opened it and stepped inside, then held it for them all to enter. A young man who looked younger than Neil glanced up from the computer in front of him.

"Mickey, this is Team Camelot," Wally said. "Where's Nancy at?"

"Ladies' room," the boy said. "She should be back any minute." He stood and extended a hand to Noah. "Camelot, right? Heard a lot about you, it's a pleasure to finally meet you."

Noah shook hands with him, and then the others did

likewise. "Pleasure is mine," he said. "I understand you've been working on some things to help us with our new mission?"

"Yeah," the boy said, nodding. "Nancy is the actual brains, here. I just do what she tells me, putting all the pieces together."

"Don't let him fool you," said a feminine voice. A blonde woman in her thirties stepped into the room behind them. "I come up with some ideas, but Mickey refines them. We're a pretty good team, but I doubt either of us could accomplish much on our own. Every project we do is a collaboration."

"Which is why I trust them with the important stuff," Wally said. "All I have to do is tell them what the situation is, and then they start bouncing the ideas back and forth. Before you know it, they've invented something so new and exciting that we have to keep them completely under wraps. If any of our enemies ever found out just how bright these two are, they'd do whatever it takes to steal them away."

Nancy burst out laughing. "I hope you're all aware that Wally tends to exaggerate."

"Just show them what you've got," Wally said. "I haven't seen this stuff yet, either, so we can all make up our minds together."

Nancy nodded at Mickey, and he reached over to pick up a small plastic box off his desk. It was about the size of a ring box, but when he opened it up, they saw what looked like a small plastic rod.

"This is the latest thing in subdermal trackers," he said. "It works like a contraceptive implant, just under the skin. 433 megahertz, ultrahigh frequency RFID chip inside." He pointed at three small, round devices that were still on his desk. "These units can read the chip from up to half a mile away, or up to 1500 feet through brick and concrete. If you set them around the area where the women's prison is located within the compound, they'll triangulate its position within only a few inches. Each one has a battery that's good for about two weeks of continuous use. We'll give you these to practice with during your training, but when it comes down to the real mission you will have fresh units with new batteries."

He picked up something else from the desk. This time it was a device that looked like a common tablet computer. "This is the monitor that receives the encrypted data from the scanners and translates it into an image it can display on a tactical blueprint of the prison, with every room and section marked. That way, you'll know exactly where Sarah is at all times."

Noah nodded his head. "Okay," he said. "That'll definitely help when it's time to get her out."

"Exactly," Nancy said. "But that isn't all we've got for you." She nodded to Mickey again.

"The rest isn't quite as high-tech as that," the young man said, "but it should come in handy." He held out another small box, this one containing three devices that looked like small plastic cones. "These little gadgets, when you place them against a wall, can detect movement on the other side. They're fairly simple, because all they do is pick up vibrations transmitted through the wall. That could be vibrations from someone speaking, or somebody walking along, just about anything. Even the sound of someone breathing will create tiny vibrations in the walls that can be detected. They are ultrasensitive, but only in the direction they're focused. You can be talking while you're holding it, and it won't even notice."

"You can use these to make sure a room is empty before you enter it," Nancy added. "You just hold the big end against a wall or door, and watch the needle on the smaller end. If it moves at all, there is something on the other side that's causing vibrations. You can get an idea of the type of vibration, as well, by watching the needle. People walking will be rhythmic, people talking will be erratic and fluctuate. Breathing will be rhythmic, but soft."

Mickey nodded. "You'll get the hang of it pretty quickly," he said, then stepped around his desk to a workbench and picked up what looked like a toy submachine gun. "Now, this little baby will come in handy when you go in, and especially if you encounter resistance. It fires a gel capsule filled with a gas at surprisingly high pressure. The gas is derived from scopolamine, and a single whiff of it is enough to render someone essentially motionless for several minutes. It doesn't knock them out, but it inhibits thought and intention. Basically, anybody who gets a sniff of it suddenly can't remember what they were doing or think of anything else to do, so they just stop wherever they're at and do nothing until it wears off. A side effect is that they usually won't remember anything from the last few minutes before it hit them until the point where they realize they've been out of it, so they won't even be aware they've been affected. We'll also give you some little sticks of chewing gum that act as an antidote, so it won't affect you even if you walk through a cloud of it."

"Chewing gum?" Neil asked.

"Yes," Mickey said. "The antidote is embedded in it, and it is absorbed rapidly into the bloodstream through the tissues under your tongue. We're talking like within one or two seconds, that fast."

"Okay," Noah said. "And how long does the effect last,

once we shoot somebody with these?"

"The immobility will last seven to nine minutes, so you'll have to move pretty quickly once you use it. We've got three of these ready for you, and they each hold about 120 shots."

Neil grinned. "So, we just shoot somebody in the face with it?"

Mickey chuckled at him. "You don't even have to hit them. The gas will spread out quite a ways, so if you hit the wall anywhere near them, they're going to get a sniff. The guns are set for three round bursts, and even one burst can stop a small group of people."

"How accurate are they?" Noah asked. "Do you have any dummy rounds we can practice with?"

"Actually, yes," Mickey said. "I figured you'd want to get the hang of them, so we made up a thousand rounds with just air inside. The gel capsules burst on impact with anything, because the pressure inside is just barely low enough to keep them from bursting on their own."

Noah nodded. "Okay, so we can keep track of where Sarah is at inside the prison all the time, we can scan a room for occupants before we enter it and we can incapacitate anyone who gets in the way. What about a way for her to let us know when she's made contact with her target?"

Nancy smiled and took a step closer to Noah. "Well, that presented a bit of a problem, because there's no way she can take any sort of communication device in with her. We thought about adding a transmitter to the implant, but anything that emits an active radio signal is likely to be detected and might even expose her. I was forced to resort to desperate measures, so I just told Mickey there was no possible way we could accomplish it."

Wally let out a loud guffaw. "Telling Mickey something can't be done is a surefire way to get it accomplished. Right, Nancy?"

She nodded, still smiling. "Exactly," she said. "Mickey came up with the idea of yet another little implant, one that will emit a signal just once. The same receivers that triangulate the tracker will receive that signal, letting you know that she's ready for extraction."

Sarah spoke for the first time. "You guys sure get off on shoving stuff into my body," she said. "Are you certain none of this will hurt me?"

"Not a bit," Nancy said. "We've got some anesthetic gel that will keep you from even feeling it when we implant them. The tracker is going into your right thigh, and the extraction signal..."

"I call it the panic button," Mickey put in.

"Okay, the panic button will be inserted just under the skin outside your left rib cage. You'll be able to feel it with your fingers, and all you have to do to set it off is press it until it snaps. You'll be able to tell when you got it done, and your team will get the signal to come snatch you out."

Sarah gave her a sour grin. "Okay, so when do you stick me with this stuff?"

"Oh, not until you're ready to go. We've got some made up that won't be actually implanted for you to use during your training." She nodded at Mickey, who picked up a larger plastic box and passed it to Sarah. "There are three panic buttons and one tracker in there. They have tape on them, just stick them to yourself. Other than that, they work just like the real one. Camelot, you'll use the scanners and monitor during training, so that you get the hang of them."

Noah nodded. "Set us up, then," he said. "We need to get started on the practice runs today."

Wally grinned at them. "Hold on," he said, "not so fast. We got a couple other little surprises for you. Follow me."

He led them through a series of hallways and into yet another room. An older, balding man rose from his seat as they entered.

"Jeremiah, this is Team Camelot. Noah, this is Jeremiah. Whenever we run into a need for a special tool, he's the guy we come to."

Noah shook hands with Jeremiah, who smiled softly.

"Pleased to meet you," the older man said. "Wally briefed me on your mission and told me to think about what tools you might need. I managed to get a copy of the blueprints of the prison, and started thinking about what might be required if you had to create your own way in." He turned to a large table where the blueprints were laid out. "Looking at what we got on their security, it appears to me there are numerous places where it would be possible to literally cut through a wall or roof to gain entry. The trick to that, of course, is how to do so without attracting a lot of attention. Now, I looked at every angle I could think of, including the possibility of going in from under the building. It has a basement level, but that would require digging. Any kind of excavation would be pretty difficult to keep hidden unless you started some distance away and constructed a tunnel. For that reason, I decided to look at simply going through the building itself."

He pointed at various places on the designated walls near the women's section. "These are spots where I think it would be possible to cut through the wall and make an entry point, but the problem is that such an entry would be difficult to conceal. On the other hand, if you take a look at the top of the building," he added, as he flipped the blueprint away to show what appeared to be a large print of a satellite photo, "there are some pretty big sections that aren't easily observable by security. According to our intelligence, these areas that I've marked aren't even subject to video surveillance."

He turned away from the table and stepped over to a workbench where numerous tools were laid out. The first item he picked up looked like a simple tube about twenty inches long and three inches in diameter. "This is an air-launched grapple and rope. When you press the trigger button here near the bottom, compressed air shoots out a folding grappling hook that trails fifty feet of high-strength nylon line behind it. At the places I marked on that photo, that's enough for you to shoot it onto the building where it will catch on the architecture. You can then use the rope to climb up and onto the roof. The grappling hook is made of a very strong plastic and coated in rubber. It shouldn't make a very loud noise when it lands on the roof."

He set the tube back on the table and picked up the next item, a cordless drill with what looked like a sock hanging off the side, and fitted with a twenty-four-inch drill bit. "This started out as a standard cordless drill, the kind you can buy in any hardware store, but I've made a few modifications to it. The bit, on the other hand, is my own design. You can drill straight through up to twenty-four inches of wood, brick or concrete, but the length of the bit is based on spiral cutting technology. The long spiral you see that runs the whole length of it is essentially a cutting blade. Once you've drilled through, you can simply push the drill sideways and cut out a large section of whatever you drilled through. You'll be surprised at how quickly it works, and how silent it is, but the best feature is that I've added a small but extremely powerful vacuum attachment. All of the dust will be sucked up and blown into this sock, so it won't be falling into the room and giving away what you're doing."

Noah took the drill and looked at it closely. "So, as long as we pick a room with nobody in it, we should be able to cut through without being noticed?"

Jeremiah nodded his head. "Our intelligence indicates that their security doesn't use vibration detection. That being the case, it's a safe bet that if you can find an empty room and enter through the roof, no one will be the wiser. And, just to help keep it that way, I came up with a couple other little gizmos." He took the drill back from Noah and set it on the table, then picked up what looked like a six-inch-wide roll of duct tape. "This tape will stick to absolutely anything, and I've tested it on every type of material you're likely to find in that building. When you make your first straight cut, put a strip of this tape on it. Then, when you make a parallel cut, you can use another strip to secure a couple of these flat metal bars to keep that side from falling through, so that the first strip of tape will act as a hinge. That'll make a simple trapdoor that you can close behind you. Unless someone looks up and pays close attention, your point of entry should go completely undetected."

Noah looked at the tape and bars, then turned to Wally. "I think I like this guy," he said.

FOUR

The training center occupied several thousand acres to the northwest of Kirtland, and was surrounded by some of the most impenetrable fence in the world and under a no-fly zone so it could not be observed from above. Inside its borders, mission planners could construct mockups of any building or urban area, any sort of terrain and even create limited modifications to the climate. The main gate looked like the entrance to a military reservation, which is how it appeared on maps. Entry was restricted to E & E personnel or other government employees who might be temporarily attached.

The guards on the gate were just as meticulous as the ones at the R&D center, carefully examining the identification Noah and his team presented before allowing them to pass. One of the guards handed Sarah, who was driving, a quickly printed map that showed them where to go.

They drove along a wooded lane for more than three miles, and the quickly constructed mockup of the Bangkok prison came into view. It was built of wood that was covered with a sprayable plaster, so that it resembled the concrete building it was based on.

A guard shack just outside the front entrance housed

two men, one of whom stepped out as they parked the car and got out. Noah showed his ID, and the others produced their own.

"I'm Camelot," he said. "We're supposed to start our mission training today."

"Yes, Sir," the guard said, "we've been expecting you. My name is Jason, I'm supposed to give you a tour right away, and then let you set up your training as you like."

"Sounds good. Lead the way."

The guard, a stocky redheaded man in his mid-thirties, turned and led them toward the front entrance of the big building. "This is the main entrance to the women's section," he said. "There's an administrative office inside here, with holding cells for incoming inmates. We've got it staffed with actors, just ignore the fact they're not necessarily ethnically correct, okay?"

Noah and the others followed Jason into the building. There was a counter set up with four people behind it, whom Jason told them were acting as intake personnel. Once they began their training, Sarah would actually go through the intake process just the way she would when the mission began.

From there, Jason led them into the main building of the women's prison. Laid out just like the real thing, they saw a long hallway with doors off either side. Some of the doors led to medical facilities, feeding facilities, work and day rooms, while the rest went into large rooms covered with mats on the floor. The work and day rooms held a number of women who simply looked at them.

"In the actual prison, the women sleep on these mats and are all crowded together. From what we've been told, they'll be literally crowded up against each other throughout the night. Only the cell bosses, inmates who are designated to hand out work assignments and such, get any space for themselves."

Next to each of the large cells was another room that contained lockers. Each inmate, they were told, was assigned a locker, but there was no way to secure them. "Anything you stick in a locker is likely to be stolen," Jason said. "Most of the women keep anything important to them hidden inside their clothes or in their pockets, but that doesn't guarantee it won't be stolen. Most of them are lucky to hold onto their toothpaste, from what we were told."

The tour continued through other parts of the building that were normally not accessible to inmates. Noah, Neil and Marco would have to familiarize themselves with those passages, since they would probably be part of the path they would have to take when it came time to break Sarah and Sharon Ingersoll out. There were many twists and turns, and many rooms that were commonly used only by the prison staff. These included offices, storage rooms, locker rooms and a separate dining area.

"One thing I found interesting," Jason said, "is that they apparently don't use any video cameras inside the prison. The only place they have any video cameras as part of their security system is in the intake office and in the visiting areas. Other than that, they just don't bother."

Noah nodded his head. "That is interesting," he said, "but it's also good to know."

When the tour was concluded, they went back out to the guard shack. Jason showed them a room there that they could use for planning and staging their training, then left them to begin working out the details.

"Well," Noah said, "we might as well get started. Sarah, I'll walk you in as if you were being dropped off at the prison, then the guys and I will start setting up the trackers. Within a couple of hours, we'll be able to follow you all around the building."

"Okay," Sarah said. "I'm assuming there's somebody in there playing Sharon? I'll do what I can to find her, and try to work it out so that we're both in the same place at some point, so you'll know where and when to pick us up." She turned to one side and affixed the tracker to her leg, then lifted her shirt enough to put one of the temporary panic buttons on her left side. "Guess I'm ready."

Noah took hold of her arm and walked her out of the room, through the guard shack and up to the front door of the building. There was a doorbell button beside the door, and he pressed it.

A gruff-looking woman opened the door and peered out. "Yes?"

"New prisoner for you," Noah said.

The woman looked Sarah over, then reached out and took hold of her other arm. She dragged her through the door without saying another word. The door closed in Noah's face, and he turned and went back to the planning room.

Marco had found a detailed map of the building and laid it out on the table. He looked up as Noah entered. "Okay, boss man," he said, "I've been going over the blueprints. If you take a look at these plans, I think you'll see the best place to put our sensor units is here, here and here." He pointed at three different places on the drawing of the surrounding area.

"Looks good," Noah said. "Let's get them set up, and then see how well they work." he picked up the small case that held the relay units and the others followed him out the door.

It took a few minutes to orient themselves and determine where they wanted to set them up, but it was done within a little more than an hour. Neil pulled out the monitor and turned it on, and a red dot appeared on an overlay of the inside of the women's prison.

"Got her," he said. "Looks like she's in one of the holding cells in the intake section."

"It's working, then," Noah said. "Now all we have to do is wait for her to make contact with the target."

They went back to the planning room and settled into some chairs. Neil kept one eye on the monitor, and reported periodically as the red dot moved from place to place on the overlay. "Looks like they put her straight to work," he said at one point. "She's in one of the workrooms, the second one we saw. I think it was full of sewing machines, wasn't it?"

Marco nodded. "Yeah, it looked like they were making the prison uniforms there."

Noah said nothing, instead just continuing to recline in his chair.

* * *

The gruff woman had taken Sarah directly into one of the holding cells and pushed her inside. There were no other prisoners in it, and its only furnishing was a bench so she sat down to wait. The staff actors went about whatever they were doing for an hour, leaving her to sit and wait, but finally she got frustrated.

"Hey," she called out. "This is only training, we don't have to make it that realistic, do we?"

A couple of the actors looked up at her, but then looked away. It was nearly half an hour later before the same woman pulled her out of the cell and plopped her into a chair beside a desk. For the next twenty minutes, she answered questions about her name, where she lived, what she was doing in Thailand, etc. When that was finished, another woman grabbed her arm without warning and yanked her up out of the chair, then marched her through the hallway and into the shower area. She was handed a uniform and told to strip, put her personal clothing into a basket and then shower before putting the uniform on.

Sarah rolled her eyes, but did as she was told. The basket with her clothing disappeared while she was in the shower, so she put on the uniform and sat on the bench beside the shower entrance until one of the women came for her again.

This one simply told her to follow, and led her to one of the workrooms. "See that big gal with the short hair? She's the work boss. Go tell her you're here to work." The woman pushed her inside and shut the door behind her.

Sarah walked up to the woman who seemed to be in charge and said, "I'm supposed to tell you I'm ready to work."

The woman glared at her. "Then get to work," she said sarcastically. "Go around to every station and pick up the finished clothes, then sort it out by size and put it on the racks." She pointed at some wheeled shelving units.

Sarah looked around and saw that several of the women running sewing machines had stacks of finished pants and shirts on their tables, so she began gathering them up. None of them had size tags, so she was forced to simply hold them up and guess at which shelf they went on, but no one corrected her.

On her second pass around the room, she asked several of the women if they knew an American girl named Sharon, but each of them simply shook her head. She kept working for a couple of hours, and then the work boss blew a whistle. The workday had apparently come to an end.

The other women lined up by the door, and a moment later it was opened. Sarah got into line and followed them as they went into one of the day rooms. There was a television on one wall, but hardly anyone was watching.

The workroom had held about forty women, but there were more than a hundred in this room. She began asking around about Sharon once again, and finally one younger woman looked at her and frowned.

"I'm Sharon Ingersoll," she said. "Who are you?"

Sarah grinned at her. "Believe it or not, I'm here to get you out. I need you to stay as close to me as possible, so that I can signal my team to come and get us. Is there any way to know whether we'll be sleeping in the same room?"

"Sharon" shrugged. "If you haven't had a room assigned, then you can go into any of them. Just follow me, and maybe no one will say anything." She looked Sarah up and down. "I had a visitor recently who said something about maybe getting me out of here, but they didn't say how or when. How do I know you're telling the truth? I've never seen you before, you could be somebody they planted here to try to get close to me."

Sarah glanced around before she answered. "Let's just say you and I have some of the same friends," she said. "My bosses say that your bosses want you back pretty badly, bad enough to send us to get you."

The girl looked at her closely for another moment. "Do you know how hard it would be to get us out of here? We're pretty much always surrounded, either by guards or other inmates. You see those guards over there? Those little clubs they carry hurt like hell if they hit you with them. Unless you've got a squad of Marines out there somewhere, I don't see how this could work."

Sarah gave her another grin. "Trust me," she said, "the guys I've got make a squad of Marines look like Girl Scouts. We just need to pick the right time and place for them to come get us. Anybody gets in their way will wish they hadn't."

Sharon didn't change her expression, but cocked her head to one side. "The guards change shifts at midnight," she said. "They lock our doors and almost all of them disappear for about fifteen minutes or so, then the new ones come in. They don't actually come into the room, but there's always two or three of them outside each door. During shift change, that drops to one or two in the whole hallway. That would be the perfect time, if you're for real."

Sarah nodded at her. "Is there any kind of clock or anything in the rooms? Some way we can know that it's getting close to shift change?"

"No clocks," the girl said, "but they lock our doors about ten minutes before. Would that be enough advance notice?"

"I guess it'll have to be," Sarah said. "What do we do until then?"

"We hang out here for a while, then they take us to eat. I'll warn you now, the food really sucks. As soon as we're finished eating, we go to the bunk rooms. Stay close to me then, and if nobody drags you away then maybe we can get a couple of mats together. Everybody just sits on them for a while, talking and such, then when the lights go out we all have to be quiet."

"Good. Then as soon as they lock that door, I'll signal the guys to come get us."

FIVE

J ason came into the planning room at a little after four and told Noah that he was about to leave for the day. "The new shift is coming on," he said, "but they won't bother you. You guys hungry?"

"We're getting there," Noah said. "Is there someplace around here to grab some supper?"

Jason grinned. "It's about half a mile away," he said. "I'm running over there now. Want one of you guys to follow and bring back something to eat?"

"Good idea," Noah said. "Marco, you mind?"

Marco grinned. "First thing you and I ever did was go have breakfast together, remember? I never turn down the chance to eat."

Neil tossed him the keys to the Hummer, and he followed Jason out the door. He was back forty minutes later with cheeseburgers and fries, and three big cups of root beer, so the three of them cleared the table and sat down to eat.

Neil continued to watch the monitor, calling out when Sarah had left the day room and gone to eat her own dinner, then again when she ended up in one of the sleeping rooms. It was nearly 6:30 by then, and she was completely stationary after that.

At ten o'clock, Neil began yawning, so Noah told him to kick back and try to get some sleep. He took over watching the monitor, and Marco leaned back in his own chair. Ten minutes later, both of them were snoring softly.

* * *

When they left the chow hall, Sarah followed Sharon to the sleeping room without incident, and they were able to grab two pads side-by-side. She had no idea what time it might be, but knew it was still fairly early in the evening. The two of them sat and talked for a while, occasionally talking with some of the other women around them, but most of them were pretending to not speak English.

Sarah was amazed at the intensity with which most of the actors employed in the training facility played their parts. A few of the women claimed to be Americans who had been railroaded on drug charges, but most were playing native Thai or Cambodians. She heard about "ya-ba," the local name for the methamphetamines that were the most common drug charge, and witnessed some of the bullying that went on among the inmates.

Sharon had explained to her about the way some inmates abused others. "The ones that look all Butch, those are the Toms," she said. "The rest are Dees or neutrals. You can tell the difference because the neutrals don't bother to pretty themselves up. The Toms and the Dees are lesbians, but you won't see them up to anything in here. They tend to find some kind of privacy when they want to get mushy, and I'm glad of that. Sometimes, though, the Toms will just pick on any of the girls, just to be mean. I try to stay out of their way and not get their attention."

Sarah looked her over briefly. "I take it you're a neutral?"

"Yep. If anyone tries to give you nail polish, turn it down. As soon as you put it on, you're fair game."

Sarah shuddered. "Thanks for the tip, I'll remember it."

* * *

Noah was watching the monitor when it suddenly began beeping. That was the signal, he knew, telling him that Sarah had activated the "panic button."

"Heads up," he called out. "We're ready to move."

Neil and Marco came awake almost instantly, and Noah pulled the blueprint back onto the table. He pointed at a blank wall on the outside of the building, one of the places Jeremiah had selected, that seemed to be the back wall of the storage room. "We'll go up onto the roof right here," he said. "Grab the tools and guns and let's get going."

The tools Jeremiah had provided were in a bag that had been provided by R&D. The section of wall he had pointed out was about 400 yards from the main entrance, in a dimly lit area. Since the outer perimeter structure of the prison was a single-story building made of mostly just concrete and steel, there wasn't much of an alarm system on the outer walls, but as Jeremiah had suggested, they planned to scale the wall and cut down through the roof. Noah had already marked out a path he hoped to follow to where Sarah was sleeping, but he had no idea how long it would take to get to her, or what obstacles might be in the way.

They made it to the wall without being spotted, and Marco used the air-powered launcher to shoot the grappling hook up onto the roof. It caught on a lip that ran along the edge of the wall, and he went up it hand over hand. Noah followed the same way, and once they were both on the roof, the two of them pulled Neil up.

There, they hit the jackpot. A skylight looked down into the storeroom, letting them see that the room was empty, but it had alarm contacts on three sides. Raising it would set off an alarm, so Marco began drilling a hole in the roof a couple of feet away from it. Once the bit had punched through, he began moving it sideways to cut a square hole big enough for them to drop through.

Noah used some of the wide, thick tape along that side to create a hinge, then used more of it to apply the little metal bars that would prevent it from falling in, creating a way to let the cut-out panel close over them. When they got it open, they were able to lower themselves onto the top of a shelving unit, then climb quietly down to the floor. The section they had cut out was still in place, held up by the tape and bars so that it wasn't noticeable unless someone looked very closely.

"Chewing gum," Noah whispered, and each of them put a stick of gum into their mouths and began chewing. While they were not using the real gas rounds during their practice, Mickey had told them that the genuine, antidote-laced gum would protect them from the gas in their guns for up to an hour, and they didn't plan on needing it to last any longer than that.

Noah and Marco pressed the vibration-detecting cones against the inner wall that bordered the hallway, but they didn't seem to register any vibrations. The doorway that led into the room was locked from the inside, requiring a key to open it from the hallway side. Noah turned the lock quietly and pulled it open enough to peek out into the hallway. He saw no one, so he opened the door wider and glanced in both directions.

A single guard was walking away from them down the

hallway, some distance away. Noah froze until she had turned a corner, then motioned for Neil and Marco to follow as he stepped out.

Neil was holding the tablet, and held it up so Noah could see the overlay. Based on where they had entered the building, Sarah was about 200 yards away from their position, and they would have to follow the current hallway fifty yards before turning left.

Moving as stealthily as they could, they made their way to the first turn. Noah leaned out for a split second to look down the hallway, then used hand signals to tell the others that there were three people in the hallway they had to follow. As soon as he conveyed that information, he turned the corner and began moving quickly toward the three guards he had seen.

One of them noticed him and started to speak, but Noah squeezed the trigger on the gun he was holding. The gun burped softly several times, and about a dozen of the little gel rounds shot out, striking the guards and the wall behind them. The practice rounds were empty, of course, but the actors had all been coached on how to react to them. Almost instantly, they froze, simply standing where they were and staring in his direction.

The three men slipped past them, ignored by the guards. The monitor led them to another turn, this time to the right, and once again Noah peeked around the corner.

There were only two guards standing in the hallway, so Noah stepped out and fired at each of them quickly. Just like the ones before, they simply seemed to lose interest in anything and stood where they were.

One of them was standing just in front of the room where they expected to find Sarah. Noah stepped up to the barred door and looked inside, but it was dark and all he could make out were many forms lying on the mats.

"Sarah?" Noah said in a loud whisper, and he saw her rise quickly from a spot near a corner. A second woman got up with her, and they began hurriedly making their way toward the door. Unfortunately, that meant stepping over and occasionally on other inmates, who began complaining loudly. Noah tapped the bars with his gun, and most of them quieted down.

Marco was looking at the lock on the door, and turned to the guard standing nearby. A quick pat down found a ring of keys, and he began trying them in the lock. There were eleven keys on the ring, and it was the ninth one he tried that finally opened it.

Sarah and Sharon stepped out, but suddenly the lights came on and an alarm sounded. Noah glanced back down the hall and saw a number of guards rushing in their direction.

"Busted!" one of the guards shouted. "A little too much noise. No luck this time, you're going to have to try again."

Noah and the others lowered their guns as they were surrounded by the female guards. This first attempt had met with failure, but Noah had expected as much.

"We got farther than I expected," he said. "To be honest, I figured we'd have been caught quicker than this."

One of the women grinned at him. "If you'd been a few minutes quicker, you probably would've gotten away with it. Our shift change takes about fifteen minutes. I might've known your girl would think that was a good time to try the escape, but you have to move a lot faster if you plan to use it in the real mission."

Noah nodded his head. "Good advice," he said. "Let's reset, and try it again."

The guard nodded. "Okay," she said. "Go back out and let's call it a signal in fifteen minutes." She looked at Sarah. "I'm guessing you sent the signal when they locked you down?"

Sarah nodded. "Yeah," she said. "Sharon said that happened about ten minutes before the shift change, and that we have about fifteen minutes with reduced guards once it began."

"That's correct," the guard said. "Realistically, it's probably a good plan. Fifteen minutes, okay?"

Sarah and Sharon went back to their pads while the guards who were leaving their shift came back into the hallway. Noah, Marco and Neil walked out without interference, and went back to the planning room. Neil was watching the time on the monitor so that they would know when it was time to start again.

"Now," he said when it was time. Once again, they took off toward the same wall and Marco shot the grappling hook onto the roof. Up he went, followed by Noah, and then Neil, and they went through the motions of cutting through the roof again.

This time, since they were already familiar with the route, they moved a little more quickly. They made it to the sleeping room after encountering the same number of guards, then got the door open and let the two women out. Some of the other inmates began clamoring to be released as well, but Noah shut the door and locked it before any of them could get out.

Noah had studied the blueprints of the building well, and decided not to follow the same path back to the storeroom. He gave Sarah and Sharon each a stick of gum, then took off in a different direction and cut into another hallway, where he had to shoot two more guards. They hurried past them, then made two more turns without running into other guards. The last turn took them back into the hallway with the storeroom, and they slipped inside and shut the door quickly, locking it behind them.

Marco went up the shelving unit and out onto the roof first, then reached down to help Neil and the two women. Noah came up last, just as an alarm began to sound below them.

It was only about twenty-five feet to the ground, so Marco swung himself over and hung by his hands for a moment before dropping. Noah tossed the rope over to him, and Sarah, Sharon and Neil slid down it as quickly as they could. Noah waited until Neil was down and off the rope, then tossed it down, slid over the side and dropped the way Marco had done.

Guards were beginning to come out the front entrance, but they seemed disorganized. Noah led the group into the darkness, and they made it undetected to the side of a building a short distance away from the prison.

Guards were moving toward them, but they seemed to be paying more attention to the prison building itself than anything else. Noah led the group deeper into the lane beside the smaller building, and found a spot behind it for them to hide. A few minutes later, still undetected, he declared the rescue a qualified success.

"We got them out of the prison," he said, "so I think we've got the basis of a plan. The trick is to cut our trapdoor ahead of time, that will save us several minutes when the actual rescue takes place."

Neil grinned, but Marco expressed some doubt. "Do you really think it'll work in the real situation? Maybe we should think about trying some other scenarios, maybe at different times of the day or going in from different access points."

Noah turned to look at him. "I don't think so," he said. "The whole point of this mockup is that it's designed to look and operate as much like the real prison as possible. I don't know how they got information about building security, or about the shift changes and how they work, but it's almost certain that this is just the way it is in the real one. I'd rather have one concrete plan and refine it by running through it over and over than try to have multiple plans and run the risk of confusing parts of them when it comes down to the wire. That shift change is likely to be the best opportunity we're going to get, so we need to keep working on it until we've got this down to the level of ballet choreography."

Marco grinned and shook his head. "You're the boss, Boss. I'm just here to do what you tell me."

"That's exactly what you're supposed to do."

SIX

Since Noah had chosen the midnight shift change as his target opportunity, the actors and staff of the prison agreed to stop paying attention to the real hours of daylight and keep running the shift change scenario over and over. Noah called a halt to their simulations for the night, and they all bunked down in the planning room to get some sleep.

The following morning, they began running the shift change scenario in earnest. Noah gave Sarah her cell phone to use as the signaling device and sent her back into the mockup to get ready. She and Sharon would bunk down together in a simulated "lights out" situation, while Noah, Neil and Marco ran through multiple scenarios on how to get her and the target out in the least amount of time possible.

That meant trying other avenues of entry, but by the time they ran the tenth simulation, he decided that his instincts the first time had been correct. Going through the roof over the storeroom was the quickest and most effective way to get into the building. Interestingly, the actors playing the staff of the prison didn't even figure out how they were getting in until the third attempt, but they continued to act as if they knew nothing, of course.

The prison staff scheduled their mock shift changes at random times, so that they would not know when to expect the signal. As soon as the cell door was locked, Sarah would hit the speed dial to Noah's phone, let it ring once and end the call.

Simple as it was, the system worked. After fifteen practice runs, they knew each turn by heart and could use the vibration detection cones well enough to tell how many people were in the hallway outside the storeroom, and whether they were to the left or right of the door. That made it extremely easy to know when and how quickly to move.

Both Neil and Marco occasionally had to use their guns, and both of them were proficient enough for them to be effective. After the first few runs, Noah settled on putting Marco at the rear with himself on point, leaving Neil in the middle. Neil was authorized to fire anytime he thought one of the others didn't see a target, or just to make sure the targets got hit. Noah had to caution him about giggling a couple of times, but after that he became as silent and stealthy as the others.

Noah wasn't ready to quit, however. They caught a few hours of sleep Tuesday night, then continued practicing all the way to Wednesday evening. When he finally called a halt, Sarah shouted, "Hallelujah!"

They had made twenty-seven practice runs, and Noah was confident that they had greatly improved their chances of success during the real mission. He declared a holiday for the next day, and even though the weather was pretty cool, he invited them all out on the boat on Thursday afternoon.

Marco had asked if he could bring a date, and they arrived at just before noon. "Noah, Sarah," he said, "this is

Renée. She's cool, she works out at R&D in the administrative offices there. Renée, this is Noah and Sarah."

Renée was about thirty, a little older than Marco's twenty-seven, and she wasn't what you might consider a pretty woman, but she had a personality that could light up a dark room. "Oh, my gosh," she said. "I've heard so much about you guys, it's a pleasure to finally get to meet you."

"Same here," Noah said, but Sarah took to her instantly.

"Pleasure's all mine," she said. "Nice to have another girl around, what with all this testosterone. You guys been dating long?"

"About six months, now," Renée said with a nod. "Marco was assigned to us for a couple of weeks, helping out with some equipment testing, and we just sort of hit it off. When he found out he was being assigned to your team, he called me up and took me out for a steak dinner to celebrate. You're pretty much all he's talked about since then."

Neil and his girlfriend Lacey came walking over from his trailer a few minutes later, and Renée was introduced to them. Moments later, the three girls were chatting away as if they'd known each other for years. Noah watched them for a moment, then he and the other two guys grabbed a couple of coolers full of lunch and soft drinks and led the way down to the boat house.

The sun was up and shining, but the air temperature was only in the mid-sixties when they started the boat and headed out onto the lake. Noah cruised along slowly, trying to avoid giving them a chill, but the steady breeze made them keep their jackets on. When they were about half a mile from shore, he shut down the engine and let the boat drift. The six of them sat out in the breeze for a little while, but then moved into the cabin.

Sarah turned on the radio and let the local rock station play in the background as they sat and talked. Renée broke the ice by telling them a few funny stories about Marco's time in R&D.

"Marco was sent to us to help in testing some equipment they were developing," she began, "but nobody told him what it was. When he got there, Wally just dropped him off at one of the workshops and told him to do whatever they needed him to. He was all excited about getting to be part of the operation, so when the techs told him to put on this jumpsuit, he thought it was something to wear while he was working. Then they told him to stand in a particular spot and handed him a helmet with a face mask."

"You do know this is going to embarrass me, right?" Marco said.

"Shut up, it's funny. Anyway," she went on, "the tech told him to stick his hands in his pockets and try not to flinch, so he did, and then another tech walked up and shot him with a Taser. Well, Marco suddenly hit the floor, just about fried from the electricity, and as he lay there looking up at the two technicians, one of them looked at the other and said, 'Hmmm. It didn't work.' See, this new jumpsuit was made of some material that was supposed to keep a Taser from affecting him, but it was the first time they'd tried it on a person."

"Just for the record," Marco said, "that was the first time I ever got hit with a Taser. Did you know you pee your pants when that shock hits you?"

Neil cracked up laughing. "Oh, I wish I could've seen that!"

"I heard about it later that day," Renée said, "and it

turned out that what happened was when he was putting the suit on he didn't get it zipped all the way up. The zipper was part of the grounding or something, the thing that was supposed to make it keep the electricity away from his body, but when he didn't get it done all the way, it didn't close the circuit or whatever. So when they shot him, he got the full impact. And yes, he peed his pants."

"That's hilarious," Neil said, and both Sarah and Lacey were laughing along with him.

Marco pretended to glare at the three of them, then looked at Noah. "At least one of you isn't laughing," he said.

"Noah never laughs at anything," Neil said, "he doesn't know how. If he did, he'd be rolling on the floor about now. Oh, man, I would have loved to have been there. Next time you pick on me, I'm gonna remind you to check your diapers!"

Noah shrugged his shoulders. "I know it's funny," he said, "but humor doesn't affect me the way it does most people. It's part of that disorder I've got."

Renée turned and looked at him. "I've heard about that," she said. "You're the man with no emotions, right?"

"That's him," Sarah said. "Something happened to him when he was a kid, and his subconscious shut down all his emotional responses. Turns out that's what makes him the best at what he does. Most people, even the best-trained killer, have to deal with some kind of emotional context in every situation. Noah doesn't, so he never hesitates."

Renée looked from Sarah to Noah and back again. "But —no emotions at all? You two seem pretty close."

"We are," Sarah replied. "It's different, though, from the way most couples are. Noah knows I'm in love with him, but he can't feel the same thing for me. The best I can get out of him is an admission that he thinks things are better when I'm around, so I just take what I can get." She glanced at Noah and the look in her eyes said it all. "It works for us."

"When they told me I was being assigned to Team Camelot," Marco said, "I got the full briefing on it. Queen Allison says Noah always puts the mission first and his team second, and I can understand why that's so important in this racket. When I read through your mission reports, though, it seems to me he goes out of his way to keep all of you safe, and then there's the times he's gone to extremes to rescue you, Sarah." He looked at Noah. "You'll forgive me if that doesn't sound all that unemotional to me?"

Noah shrugged again. "I can't explain it," he said. "It's not anything I consider emotional. I just don't want to live in a world that doesn't have Sarah in it, that's all. If that means I have to take action, then I take it."

"Emotions or not," Renée said, "there's still something romantic about it. Every girl wishes she had a guy who would do whatever it took to keep her safe, right?"

Sarah and Lacey both nodded, and both of them were grinning.

"Okay, let's cut out the mushy stuff," Neil said. "Isn't anybody else getting hungry?"

Noah opened one of the coolers and began passing out ham sandwiches while Sarah opened the other and offered soft drinks around. They continued chatting as they ate, and Lacey dug her elbow into Neil's ribs.

"So," she said, "if some crazy maniac kidnapped me, would you do whatever it took to get me back?"

"Absolutely," Neil said, nodding his head. "I'd go straight to Noah and remind him that I've always been willing to help when we had to rescue his girl, so now he could help me rescue mine."

"You mean you wouldn't come rushing in with guns blazing?"

"I could do that," Neil said around a bite of his sandwich. "But with my aim, I might shoot you by mistake. Trust me, it'll be a whole lot better if I get Noah involved." He looked over at Noah. "Hey, Boss, you'd help me rescue Lacey, wouldn't you?"

Noah looked him in the eye. "Don't we always take care of our own?"

Neil turned back to Lacey and grinned. "See? Your safety is in the best possible hands."

Even in the cabin of the boat, the air was cool. The six of them finally decided to go topside and enjoy the sunshine, and were delighted to find that it had actually warmed up a bit. They cruised the lake for a couple of hours, then made their way back to the boathouse and Noah tucked the cruiser inside.

The rest of the afternoon was spent playing cards at Noah's big kitchen table, and Marco learned quickly that Noah could bluff at poker better than anyone. He lost almost a hundred dollars before he insisted they play something else, so they switched to spades. Neil and Lacey, as a team, won the first two games, but Marco and Renée took the next one.

It was nearly seven o'clock by then, so they decided to go out for dinner. There was a new restaurant that had opened in Kirtland and they all agreed to give it a try, and spent the next couple of hours just relaxing over dinner and dessert before everyone headed for home.

Noah and Sarah slept late on Friday, planning to spend the day together at home. They were awakened at ten by the ringing of Noah's phone, and he picked it up to see that it was Allison calling.

"Since you seem to be satisfied with your plans," she said, "I'm stepping up the timetable. Briefing tomorrow morning at 0900, and you will be flying out in the after-noon. You're going to lose a whole day between the flight and the time zone changes, so we need to take advantage of your early completion. Any objections?"

"No, Ma'am," Noah said. "See you at 0900."

SEVEN

"Here are your mission identities," Jefferson said the next morning. "Sarah, your name is Kayla Maguire, and you're visiting Thailand on vacation. You'll be staying at the Dream Hotel, a popular spot for American vacationers. This Wednesday evening, you'll go to the nightclub there and meet with one of our operatives to receive the drugs that will get you arrested. Later that night, your room will be raided by police and you'll be taken into custody. It should take them about three days to get you sentenced and sent over to the prison."

"Sounds like fun," Sarah said with a grimace.

"Also, in order to avoid connecting you with Noah and the rest of the team, you will be arriving in Thailand on a different flight. You'll all be leaving from Denver this afternoon at the same time, but Sarah, you will be getting on a different flight after you arrive at LAX. Noah, Marco and Neil will be on the same connecting flight together just an hour later, but your flight from LAX to Bangkok leaves two hours after theirs."

Sarah shrugged. "I'm a big girl, I can handle it. I guess this means I won't have any contact with them until the mission comes to a head?"

"That's correct, I'm afraid." Jefferson said. "Noah, you and the guys will be staying at a hotel called the Thai Cozy House, some distance from the prison. It's within signal range of your tracking units, so once you get them in place you'll be able to watch everything on your monitor tablet. Noah, you'll be Peter Allen. Marco, your name is Joshua Stevens. Neil, you're Sean Hendricks. The three of you will operate under the cover of freelance journalists, working on travel stories about Bangkok for magazines. While Sarah is going through her ordeal with the police and the jail, you'll be going to the prison and talking with the guards and staff, becoming familiar to them so you're not as noticeable."

"Wait a minute," Neil said. "We're supposed to be doing travel stories, and you want us to go to a prison?"

Jefferson nodded. "Yes. It seems that a lot of tourists, both Americans and Europeans, like to go and visit inmates at the prison. There are websites where you can choose the inmate you want to visit; it's become quite a large part of the local tourism industry. That will be the basis of your cover story, that you're doing an article on the uniqueness of visiting random strangers who are looking at ten years or more in prison."

"I've heard of that," Marco said. "Not sure I'd think it was a lot of fun, though."

"I'm sure it wouldn't be," Allison said. "It's simply a convenient fact that fits in with your need for a cover story that allows you to remain close to the prison. By the time Sarah is actually inside, you should have your tracking units in place and be ready to keep track of where she's at."

"It'll also give us a chance to get our entryway prepared," Noah said. "Since we'll be hanging around the prison a lot, we should get a decent opportunity to scout the wall we have to scale and get on the roof to cut our trapdoor out."

Allison grinned at him. "Yes, I heard about your exploits at the mockup. As far as we know, our intel on the prison and how it runs is pretty good, but don't take any unnecessary risks. Be absolutely sure no one is inside that storeroom before you start cutting your way through."

Jefferson handed them their mission kits, containing their identifications, passports, cell phones, credit cards and everything else they would need to look legitimate. The men got press cards, digital recorders and cameras, while Sarah got a purse and all the detritus that tends to collect in them.

"Incidentally," Jefferson said, "the special equipment you'll be using, including the monitor, tracking units, tools, vibration detection cones and even the special scopolamine guns, are being sent out today on a diplomatic flight to the US Embassy in Thailand. A CIA station officer there will pass it off to a local E & E operative, who will see that it gets to you, Noah, after your arrival in Bangkok."

Sarah was also given a couple of suitcases full of clothes, cheap jewelry and makeup. "Sarah, you won't be taking any of your own things with you. This stuff is destined to be confiscated when you get arrested. Noah will be provided with another set of identification materials for you by the time you need it, passport and all, as well as a set for Ms. Ingersoll, and luggage with clothing and such for both of you. Those are already prepared and waiting in Thailand."

"Speaking of her," Noah said, "is she aware of any of this? Does she have any idea someone is coming to get her?"

"Yes," Allison replied. "She got a visit from someone claiming to be an old friend—one of our operatives, of course—a couple of weeks ago, and the visitor was able to convey that information. Unfortunately, there was no way to give her a lot of details. She has no idea how soon rescue is coming, or that she'll be given a complete new identity afterward. You'll have to explain that to her after you get her out, Noah. Sarah shouldn't try to give her too much information while they're inside. There's too great a risk they might be overheard, or that too much information might be more than the girl can handle, under the circumstances. Better if she finds out the details after you get her out of there."

Noah nodded, and Sarah agreed not to try to tell the girl too much. The briefing lasted only a few more minutes, and they were told to go home and pack, then head off to the Denver airport by four o'clock. They had been out to R&D even earlier in the morning, and Sarah's implants were already in place.

Except for Sarah, each of them had driven their own vehicles to the briefing. Sarah rode with Noah, of course, and they talked on the way back to the house.

"I'm scared," Sarah said. "This mission isn't at all what I thought I signed up for. I don't know if I can handle it, Noah, not without you looking over my shoulder."

"But I will be," Noah said. "One of us will be watching that monitor every second. I'll know exactly where you are at all times, and the minute you signal us we'll be on the way in. I won't let anything happen to you."

She reached across the console and laid a hand on his arm. "That makes me feel a little better," she said, "but I won't even see you until then. Once we change planes in LA, I'm on my own. I told Allison I could handle it, but between you and me it scares the hell out of me. I've been questioned by cops before, it can get pretty intense. What if I blow it?"

"You just stay in character. Kayla Maguire would be a terrified girl in a situation like that, so it's okay to be scared. Use it, make it part of your whole performance. If they start pushing you too hard, just start crying and refuse to answer anything. I'm sure that's what they're used to, so it won't seem out of character and will give you a chance to think, pull your thoughts together."

Without warning, Sarah suddenly began chuckling. "I'm sorry," she said, "I just suddenly caught myself imagining you trying to use that technique. The thought of you ever breaking down and crying was just too much and I had to laugh."

Noah shrugged. "I probably couldn't do it if I tried, so my equivalent to that would be to simply glare at whoever was questioning me and dare them to do their worst. It's pretty much the same thing, just a way to shut out what's happening and organize my thoughts."

Sarah looked at him and cocked her head sideways. "You've actually thought about how you would do something like that, haven't you? Are you always prepared for anything?"

"No. No matter how much you try to prepare, some things will always catch you off guard. That doesn't stop me from trying, though. Whenever I'm faced with a mission, I try to imagine everything that could possibly go wrong and develop some idea of how I would handle it if it did. Most of the time, I can at least adapt a plan to fit whatever situation catches me by surprise."

Sarah shook her head but said nothing more. They rode in silence the rest of the way to the house, then Sarah led the way inside. With nearly six hours to kill, they spent some time watching a movie, but then Sarah said she wanted to lie down for a bit. Noah followed her into the bedroom, where she suddenly spun and threw her arms around him. She kissed him passionately, then tore his shirt as she was trying to take it off him.

Four hours later, as they lay in bed with their arms twined around each other, Sarah whispered, "Noah, I'm scared. What if this mission goes wrong? What if—what if this is the one I never come back from?"

"We'll all be watching over you," Noah said. "You know I won't let anything happen to you, if I can possibly prevent it."

She gave him a droll chuckle. "It's the things that you can't prevent that I worry about," she said. She twisted herself a bit so that she was looking up at his face, and propped her chin on her hands, which were on his chest. "Part of it is just that I'd hate leaving you alone. I know you're tough, I know you'd get over it, but you've kinda gotten used to me taking care of you in a lot of ways. I'd hate to just suddenly be gone."

Noah looked at her, and for a brief moment she thought she saw sadness in his eyes. "I don't want to be without you," he said. "Life is better when you're with me."

Despite her concerns, Sarah couldn't help laughing. "Considering who I'm talking to, I figure that's the equivalent of a romantic soliloquy. If you were anybody else, we'd be talking about wedding plans."

Noah cocked his head. "Would you like to?" he asked. "Get married, I mean?"

Sarah rolled her eyes. "Don't be silly," she said. "Queen Allison would have a fit, and marriage isn't something you really want, anyway."

"If you want to get married," Noah said, "then I want to marry you. I don't ever want to be with anyone else, and I don't want you to be with anyone else. Logically, that means that marriage is the type of commitment I want with you." He hooked a finger under her chin and lifted her face slightly so that she was looking him in the eye.

Sarah's eyes were wide, and her mouth was slightly opened as she tried to catch her breath, but that didn't stop Noah. He looked deeply into her eyes and said, "Sarah, will you marry me?"

She stared at him for a moment, then rolled off of the bed and walked into the bathroom. Noah heard the shower run a moment later, so he got up and followed her. She was standing under the water, just letting it run down her face and body, but she turned to look at him as he entered.

"Did you really just ask that?"

"Yes," Noah said.

She stared at him for a few seconds, and then slowly began to nod her head. "Yes," she said.

After they had showered and dressed again, she helped Noah pack his two suitcases. They would be riding to the airport in Hummer-Stein, the big Hummer that Neil used as a personal vehicle. Besides being big enough for all four of them, it had plenty of cargo space in the back for their luggage and the suitcases Sarah had been given were already loaded into it.

Packing took less than half an hour, so they were ready to go when Marco pulled in. Noah and Sarah joined him in the walk over to Neil's trailer, where the Hummer sat with its tailgate open. They put their bags inside and then Noah tapped on the trailer door.

Neil and Lacey stepped outside, and the girl put her arms around him and pulled him close. "You come back safe, you hear me?" She kissed him thoroughly, and then gently pushed him toward Noah. "He's all yours for now, but you bring him back."

Noah nodded. "I plan to."

The four of them climbed into the Hummer and Neil waved once more to Lacey as he started it up. A moment later, they turned onto the road and headed toward the highway that would take them to the interstate, and to Denver.

EIGHT

The flight to Los Angeles was brief, but Noah, Marco and Neil would have a two-hour layover before their connecting flight to Thailand. Sarah followed along with them, relieved to find that her own connecting flight left from a gate close to theirs. She would have time to see them off, and they even sat down and had a light snack before it was time to board their plane.

Both flights would last almost 20 hours, so she would be arriving a couple of hours after they did. By that time, Sarah knew, the men would already be out of the airport and in or near their hotel. Noah would want to get started on their cover stories immediately, and she knew that she was to have no contact with them before the escape.

Holding back tears, she kissed Noah goodbye when his flight was announced, then turned and walked off toward one of the small bars nearby. She turned at the last minute to see Noah disappear through the door into the boarding ramp, then entered the bar and took a seat at the counter.

"Traveling without the boyfriend?" The waitress appeared and set a glass of water in front of her. "Sorry, but I couldn't help seeing how you watched him go."

Sarah shrugged and gave her a sad smile. "Fiancé," she

said. "We both have to go out of town on business, just sucks we can't travel together."

The waitress nodded. "Yeah, it sucks. What can I get for you?"

Sarah glanced up at the board and chose a Vodka Collins. The waitress returned with it only a couple of minutes later, and left her to sip it in silence.

* * *

"She'll be okay, Noah," Neil said. "Sarah's a smart girl, she'll make it."

"She'll cry," Noah said. "She's pretty frightened about this mission, because it basically puts her on point instead of me. I gave her some tips on how to use her fear and her tears to advantage, though. By the time she actually gets into the prison, I think she'll have herself well under control."

Noah was seated at the window, with Neil beside him and Marco on the aisle. They had just stowed their carry-on luggage and taken their seats, waiting for the plane to begin to move.

Other passengers were boarding, and Noah listened to a few disputes about who was supposed to be in what seat, but none of that affected him. Neil seemed to think the arguments were funny, while Marco had earphones plugged in and was leaned back with his eyes closed.

Finally the doors were closed and Noah listened to the engines starting up. The plane was pushed back out of its parking space and the engine sounds increased until it began to move forward, swinging around to point toward the taxiway.

They moved in a start and stop pattern, slowly getting closer to their turn on the runway. It took almost 12 minutes before the plane turned into position, and then the engines began to scream as the pilot tested his brakes. A moment later he let them go, and the plane began rolling.

Noah looked out the window as the runway and scenery flashed by, and then the plane was airborne. This flight would last nearly 20 hours, landing in Taiwan for a two-hour layover before making the final flight to Bangkok. Both of the flights, though boring, were otherwise uneventful, and they arrived in Bangkok at just after five AM. Another half hour let them gather up their luggage and head for the front exit.

In order to avoid scrutiny, Noah had been told to take a taxi to the hotel, the Thai Cozy House. They selected one at random and rode along quietly. The drive took slightly more than half an hour, and then they were able to settle into their room. The room held four twin-size beds, and Neil joked about being glad he didn't have to share a bed with either of the other men.

There was a table and a desk in the room, and Neil commandeered the desk for his computers and equipment while Noah and Marco unpacked their cameras and recorders.

"Let's head over to the prison," Noah said, "and start building our cover. If at all possible, we want to get ourselves a tour of the inside."

"You think they'll let us see the women's section?" Marco asked. "Wouldn't hurt my feelings a bit to make sure it's really like the one we practiced in."

"We'll ask," Noah said. "More than anything else, though, we just want to reinforce the idea that we are trying to do a story on tourists coming to the prison. Our angle will be that visiting the inmates is an interesting experience that every American tourist coming to Bang-kok ought to try."

Marco nodded. "In that case, maybe we should actually try to interview some of the inmates. Get their perspective on having random strangers come to visit them, you think?"

"We're definitely going to try. Neil, see if you can find that website that Jefferson mentioned, pick a few names we might want to talk to. That might make it easier to get inside, too."

It took Neil only a couple of minutes to find the website, and they chose three inmates: two men, both Americans, named Albert Parker and Phillip Swan, and a woman named Angela Brown. Neil printed out the bios and photos on all three, and they locked up the room as they started toward the prison.

Visitor registration didn't open until after eight, so they made their way to a small restaurant and managed to find coffee and a fairly recognizable breakfast. By the time they got their food and were finished eating, it was already a few minutes past eight. Noah paid the tab and left a generous tip, then they made their way to the boat that would take them to the prison.

It was a little after nine by the time they finally arrived. The visitor registration office of the prison was near its front entrance, and Noah was lucky enough to find an officer there who spoke fluent English. They showed their press credentials and Noah explained that they were working on a story about tourists visiting inmates at the prison, and that they wanted to interview the three inmates they had chosen.

"We would have to get approval from the warden," the woman explained. "We get a lot of tourists who want to visit inmates, but I'm not sure the warden is going to want your cameras and recorders inside. Let me make a couple of calls, just wait here."

It was nearly 15 minutes later when she reappeared. "Sir, I got permission for you to interview these inmates, but you must submit your recordings for review before you leave. Will that be a problem?"

Noah smiled. "Not at all," he said. "Frankly, I expected as much. Don't worry, our goal is to make this sound like a fun adventure. We're not going to ask questions that might paint the prison in a bad light."

She nodded and smiled back. "Very good," she said. "Let's get you in to see your first inmate, then. The men's visiting section is full at the moment; would you mind visiting the woman first?"

"No, that would be fine."

They filled out the required paperwork and were led into the prison and to the women's visiting area. There was a waiting room where they were told to have a seat while Ms. Brown was brought in. It was nearly 30 minutes later when they were finally called inside.

They saw very little of the structure of the women's prison, so they didn't get a chance to compare it to the mockup they had trained in. The only thing they noticed was that it seemed cleaner and neater than they had expected.

They were led into a booth that was barely big enough for the three of them, facing a glass window. A large woman with short brown hair was seated on the other side, and she looked up at them with a smile, then picked up the telephone receiver on her side and pointed at the one on theirs.

Noah picked it up and smiled back at her. "Hello," he

said. "Angela?"

"Yes," Angela said with a nod. "I was surprised to hear that I was getting a visit today. How did you happen to choose me?"

"We are actually reporters," Noah said. "We're here to do a story on tourists who visit inmates, so we thought we ought to experience it. I'm Peter, and this is Josh and Sean. Do you mind if Sean records our visit on video?"

Angela's eyes went wide, but she continued to smile. "No, that's fine. Maybe you could post it on YouTube or something when you get home? I'm sure my family would love to see it."

Noah took a notepad out of his pocket. "Sure, we can do that. How would I contact them?"

She gave him her mother's email address while Neil set up the camera and taped a small microphone to the earpiece of the phone receiver. That would allow the camera to pick up her voice as well as Noah's. When he was ready, he signaled Noah to begin the interview.

"Angela Brown," Noah said. "It's a pleasure to meet you."

"No, trust me, the pleasure is all mine. You're the first visitor I've had in almost a year. My family has been here a couple of times, but it's just too expensive for them to keep coming back to visit. This was quite a pleasant surprise, being told I had a visit today."

"Well, we're glad we have the chance to brighten your day. Angela, can you tell me a bit about your story? How you came to be here, and what your sentence is, that sort of thing?"

"Sure. I'm doing a thirty-year sentence, and I've been here seven years already. It's my own fault, I got involved with some people who were doing yaba—that's the local word for meth—so when they got arrested I was rounded up with them. Don't get me wrong, I wasn't exactly innocent, but I wasn't part of the drug dealing they were into. I just happened to be there and used a bit of it myself, but in Thailand, if you're present when drug deals are happening, you're just naturally guilty with everybody else."

"Wow, thirty years? You seem to be in pretty good spirits. How are you handling it all?"

"Oh, don't get me wrong, it can get pretty depressing in here. There are days when I don't even want to get up off my pallet, but Jesus gets me through. I found Jesus about six years ago, and He helps me cope with it all. There are some missionaries that come every week and teach Bible study, so I get to spend time with them, and we pray and study God's Word. That helps me handle it."

Noah talked with her for almost half an hour, and then the phone suddenly went dead. Angela grinned and held up five fingers, mouthing the word, "Wait." Five minutes later, the phone suddenly came to life again and they were able to talk for another thirty minutes.

At that point, the visit ended and Neil unhooked the microphone and packed away the camera. The three men were led out and back to the registration area, where the same woman told them they would have to wait another hour before they could see the first of their male inmates. She collected the SD cards, promising to return them before their next visit.

There was a food stall nearby, and they decided to go and have something to drink. They found some Cokes and bought them, and then went into a small store where it was possible to buy gifts for inmates you were visiting. Angela had told them that she had to buy her own food, toothpaste, everything, so Marco decided to send her some fresh fruit and toiletries. Noah told Neil to get video of the entire transaction, keeping their cover intact.

Marco made his selections, writing down the items he wanted to purchase and then taking the list to a counter. A clerk took his money and promised to have all of the items delivered to Angela within an hour. From what she had told them, many inmates received such gifts from their visitors, and it was one of the few areas of prison life where things seemed to be done honestly. It was almost certain that everything he bought would actually get to the woman, but then it would be up to her to hang onto it and prevent it being stolen.

They returned to the waiting area and talked about their visit with Angela and the gifts they had sent her, doing their best to give the impression that the visit had deeply affected them.

It was actually closer to an hour and a half before they were called to go and visit Philip, and the first thing they noticed was that the men's side wasn't in nearly as good repair as the women's. The walls were filthy, and they noticed a lot of men wearing inmate clothing who seem to be working on construction jobs, repairing some damaged areas and even putting up a few new walls. Another man who was walking with them to the visiting area told them that these were inmates who were close to the end of their sentences. It was no longer considered necessary to keep them under maximum observation, so they were allowed to do jobs without supervision.

The visiting area was also in disrepair, and when they sat down in the booth they were able to see that the other side was quite filthy. There were stains on the wall that Noah was sure were from men urinating on them, and other stains that may have been even worse things.

A thin man sat down on the other side of the glass and picked up the receiver. Neil had already taped his microphone to the one on their side, but he didn't turn the camera on until Noah had asked permission.

"Sure," the man said. "Will this be on TV sometime?"

"That's possible," Noah said. "More likely we'll just use it as source material for an article, though. If you want, we might be able to put it on YouTube and send a message to your family so they can watch it."

"Yeah, that'd be great. I can give you my brother's email, you can send it to him."

* * *

Sarah's flight had landed while the men were having breakfast, but he wasn't aware of that. She gathered her luggage and found a limousine waiting to take her to the Dream Hotel. She had been provided with ample local currency, and the trip cost her 2200 baht, or roughly 70 dollars.

A room was already booked in the name of Kayla Maguire, and she was surprised to find that it was a very nice one. She set about unpacking, the way she expected a tourist would, and then called room service to bring her up some breakfast.

"Too bad I won't have time to get used to this," she muttered to herself. Still, it was only Monday and she didn't have to start her part of the mission until Wednesday evening, so she decided to enjoy the luxury as long as she could.

There was a large whirlpool bath, and she climbed into it as soon as she had finished breakfast. An hour of soaking in hot, bubbly water took away a lot of the stress from the flight and left her ready for some rest. She dried off and climbed into the king-size bed and drifted off to sleep while wondering what Noah was up to.

NINE

Noah, Marco and Neil spent a good part of the day visiting with the other inmates, and then managed to get a tour of the men's area of the prison while they waited for the last tape to be returned to them. An English-speaking guard led them through the facility, and told them that this was known as a "banana tour." That meant that the inmates complained that they felt like monkeys on display in a zoo, and the looks most of the prisoners gave them confirmed that theory.

"They don't like *farangs* staring at them," their guide said. "That's what we call foreigners, here. Most of our inmates are from our country or one of those nearby, and they all feel the same way. They begin to feel they are on exhibit, like they are not really people anymore."

"I can understand that," Noah said. "Most of these people are doing some pretty hard time. Back home, their sentences would be much shorter."

"That is what they tell me, at least those from the West. The British, the Americans, the Canadians—they wouldn't spend nearly as much time in prison if they had committed their crimes there. Here, though, we are much more serious about punishing the trafficking of drugs. *Yaba* destroys many lives, so it is fitting that those who produce and smuggle it into our country should pay a serious price."

Noah looked around. "But does it really help? Your prisons are as overcrowded as any in the world, and from what I understand it's almost all because of the drugs. Does it really help to make the sentences so severe?"

The guard shrugged. "There are those who believe it does not, but just as many believe that it does. I think, myself, the problem is not so much the availability of the drugs as it is the high profits they bring. In an economy where most people live below poverty level, is it so surprising that many of them will take great risks in order to reap what they consider to be great rewards?"

Noah grinned at him. "That's just about the way it is back in our country," he said. "As long as the drugs are so profitable, people will do whatever it takes to provide them to those who want them. Back home, they consider the likelihood of prison as just one of the costs of doing business."

The tour lasted a couple of hours, and then Noah and the others were led back to the front entrance. They stopped once more at the visitors' registration office and spoke with the same woman who had helped them earlier. Noah let her know that he would be coming back the next day to visit more inmates, and she smiled and told him she looked forward to seeing him again. Noah posed with her and had Neil take a couple of photographs, which made her blush and giggle.

By the time they left the prison, it was late in the afternoon. They had bought a light lunch at one of the food courts near the registration office, but it hadn't properly satisfied any of them. Neil pointed out a restaurant near where they would board the ferryboat, and Noah nodded his agreement.

The food was local Thai, and each of them tried something different. Noah had a chicken curry, Neil had what looked like kebabs with chunks of pork and vegetables, and Marco went for crab chili. Each of them was given extra dishes of rice, dips and sauces, and they were all surprised at the quantity of food. Even Neil didn't leave the table wishing for more.

Despite the fact that they had slept a lot on the flights that brought them to Thailand, all of them felt tired at the end of that day. They got back to the hotel and decided to forgo watching television in favor of stretching out on their beds and getting some sleep.

* * *

Sarah had slept until mid-afternoon, then rose and decided to act like the tourist she was supposed to be. She dug through the clothes they had given her, smiling at some and grimacing at others, but finally selected a pair of bicycle slacks and a long-sleeved top in a style she would never wear in her own persona. The weather was warm, but she got the feeling that it might rain at any time, so she opted for trainers rather than sandals, grabbed her purse and camera, and headed out to see a few sights. She found a map of tourist attractions in the hotel lobby, and was looking it over when a taxi driver approached her.

"You going sightsee?" the man asked. "I take you see all tourist attractions, very special rate. All day, all day only 3000 baht, best deal in Bangkok."

Sarah grinned at his enthusiasm, noting that he was a tiny little man. At her five foot two, she actually stood three inches taller. "Okay," she said with a giggle. "You take me to the Grand Palace?"

"Oh, yes, yes, Grand Palace very important place. Over 200 years old, very beautiful place. We go now?"

"Yep," she said, and he rushed to hold the door open for her, then did the same with the back door of his bright pink Toyota taxi. Sarah slid inside and let her eyes gaze around at the opulence of the ancient city as the driver slid in behind the wheel.

"My name Jack," he said. "I take you all around city, show you everything you want to see. We go to Grand Palace now, okay?"

"Okay," Sarah said. "Grand Palace now."

"Okay, okay," Jack said. "Grand Palace, then we go Wat Pho temple, very close. Oldest and most beautiful temple in all Bangkok! Temple of Reclining Buddha!"

He threw the Toyota into gear and they were off.

The Grand Palace was only a fifteen-minute drive from the hotel, mostly because of the number of other vehicles, bicycles and pedestrians on the road that hampered travel, but Sarah decided it was worth the wait. The massive white structure was decorated with orange and black roof tiles and gold trim on every edge, and was undoubtedly one of the most incredible buildings she had ever seen.

She was suddenly reminded of Noah's interest in architecture, and wished he was with her. She could imagine his face as he studied the logical progression of every line of the palace, and silently promised herself she'd bring him to see it, if possible, before they left Thailand.

Going through the palace took several hours, and the temple just to the south of it occupied two more. By that time, Sarah decided it was time for dinner and asked Jack to take her to a restaurant. Twenty minutes of conversation later, he delivered her to one called the Old Town Café, where she waited another twenty minutes for a table. She insisted on having Jack eat with her, which made him grin from ear to ear, and subjected her to even more of his endless chatter.

It dawned on her that she was finding his company comforting. Being without Noah for the first time in more than a year and a half, she realized she was grasping at any companionship she could find. Jack, for all his strange ways compared to her own culture, was a gentleman and his presence helped to ease her loneliness.

After dinner, Jack suggested she might want to do a little shopping, and the idea appealed to her. He took her to the Terminal 21 Mall, an extremely unusual shopping center with each floor themed after a different city. When she entered on the main level, the design reflected Paris, and she spent half an hour browsing through the many shops. One level up took her to Tokyo, or at least it seemed so. Every store and bit of artwork carried the flair of the Japanese city. When she got to the third floor, the first thing she noted was the iconic red phone booths of London, and she spent an hour browsing for souvenirs that she knew she wouldn't get to keep.

Staying in character as the carefree tourist was testing her acting ability to its limit, but she managed to keep a smile pasted on her face the whole time. When she finally declared that she was finished shopping, Jack took her to a nightclub where she actually danced with a few of the male patrons, kicking up her heels and putting on the show she knew was expected of her.

It was close to midnight by the time she got back to her hotel, and she was quite tired. She thanked Jack for a wonderful afternoon and evening, tipped him an extra 1000 baht and promised to look him up the next day if she decided to go sightseeing again. She got her room key from the desk and went up the elevator, barely concealing her disappointment at not finding any messages from Noah.

Of course, there wouldn't be. Noah was on mission, and nothing was more important to him than the mission.

* * *

A knock on their hotel room door woke Noah and the guys at about eight PM, and Noah answered it to find two young men standing there. Each of them was holding a couple of boxes, and one of them looked up with a smile. "Mr. Allen?"

"That's me," Noah said. "Can I help you?"

"Yes, Sir, we're with United News Services, Bangkok office. Apparently someone figured you needed some new cameras and recording equipment."

Noah motioned for the men to step inside, and they set the boxes on the floor. The man who had spoken looked up at Noah again as he closed the door behind them. "I'm Darrell Knapp, E & E liaison office in Bangkok. This stuff was dropped off to us yesterday, and they told us to bring it to you here tonight."

Marco produced a pocketknife packed with their camera gear and began opening the boxes. Inside one of them, they found the tracking units and the special guns they had trained with. Neil snatched up the monitor and put it with his laptop on the desk. Another held the tools they would need to cut their way through the roof over the storeroom, including two of the air-launched grappling hooks and the vibration detection cones. The other two boxes contained a carry-on bag for each of the two girls they were to take out of the prison, and new purses with identification, passports and other items relevant to their new identities.

"We appreciate it," Noah said. "How do I contact you if I need anything else?"

"I'm just a phone call away," Darrell said. He reached into his pocket and produced a business card that he handed to Noah. "Just call that number, it comes straight to my cell phone. We've been briefed on your mission, and we have the other special item all set up for you near the prison. When you're ready for it, you call that number and I'll be there to put it in the alley for you. We're keeping it in a van on life support, so once we drop it in the alley, we'll be gone."

"Understood." Noah thanked them again, and the two men left them to look through their new toys. "Looks like it's time to go to work," Noah said.

Noah and Neil used the evening to place their tracking units, concealing them carefully in bits of broken architecture on buildings surrounding the proper section of the prison. From the moment Sarah was brought to the facility, they would be able to track her every movement inside.

Fortunately, most of the sleeping areas for the women were in the same general vicinity as the one they had used in their practice runs with the mockup. No matter which one she ended up in, it would take only minor adjustments to their well-rehearsed routine to adapt to it. The only unpredictable factor was whether she would actually be able to stay close to Sharon Ingersoll once she found her. She would have to find a way to be in the same sleeping room with the girl before she used the panic button to signal them.

Marco, meanwhile, had been scouting their entry location. Just like the mockup, there were very few lights on that section of the prison structure, and he didn't see any indication of security cameras or guards. Noah had cautioned him to do nothing but scout, so he hadn't brought any tools along with him. If he had, Marco thought he could have climbed the wall and cut in the trap door on his own, without being spotted.

He had been trained to follow orders, so he had done as he was told. Had he known how easy it would be, though, he might have brought along a grapple and tools in spite of them. Marco had a habit of trying to score Brownie points with whoever was in charge, and while it had only caused minor problems in the past, he'd been written up on that issue a few times. Jefferson had cautioned him not to try it with Noah; Noah didn't think like other people, and expected his team to do exactly, and only, what they were told to do.

The three of them got back to their hotel about an hour before Sarah got to hers. They settled in for the night to get some sleep, then rose at eight the next morning and chose three more inmates to visit.

Sarah got up at about nine, and since lying in bed would be boring, she decided to find Jack and have another day of sightseeing. When things finally began, she figured it would only help her appear to be exactly what her cover claimed: a tourist who decided to be stupid and buy some drugs.

Jack had expected her, and was waiting in the lobby. When he saw her smile in his direction, he knew it was going to be another good day. Westerners, and especially the girls, tended to be generous with tips.

TEN

While Sarah was playing tourist, Noah, Neil and Marco got in a few more interviews and continue to make themselves familiar to the prison staff. Their day went smoothly, and when evening came they were ready to start preparing for the real mission.

When things happen, they tend to happen suddenly.

Sarah had stayed in her room throughout the day on Wednesday, ordering lunch and then dinner from room service. This was the day when everything would begin for her, and she wanted to be rested up before it all started. It was after seven by the time she finally decided to go down to the club, ready to begin the part of the mission that frightened her the most.

The nightclub was intense, with loud music that reminded her of some of the more extreme emo styles she had heard. She got a little table all by herself, but wasn't surprised when various men asked her to dance. Deciding she needed to keep in character, she accepted a few times, keeping an eye on the time and wondering when she would be approached about buying drugs.

At around ten, a skinny young local man asked her to dance, and didn't seem to want to take no for an answer.

She finally agreed and let him lead her onto the dance floor. It was while they were dancing that he leaned close and said, "You want *yaba?*"

For a split second, Sarah was taken aback. She had somehow expected the dealer to be an American, probably an E & E operative. She quickly realized, however, that a local made more sense, and looked at him as if curious what he was referring to.

"*Yaba,*" he said. "You call meth, maybe? Give you lots energy, make you party hard."

Sarah leaned her head to one side and gave him a grin. "Okay," she said. "How much?"

His hand dipped into a pocket and produced a small glassine envelope containing about a dozen red pills. "Special deal for you, because you pretty girl. Only 2000 baht."

With no way of knowing whether it was a good deal or not, Sarah made a show of thinking it over, then nodding her head. "Okay," she said. She stopped dancing and led the way back to her table, where she reached into her own pocket and produced the money. She counted it out into his hand, and then he slipped the envelope to her under the table.

"Okay, okay," he said. "You have good time, now." With that, he got up and left the table and Sarah watched as he exited the bar.

Staying in character for a little longer, she continued to sit at the table and finish her latest drink. When it was gone, she rose and made her way out of the club and to the elevator. She went to her room, slipped the envelope into a pocket of her suitcase, and then showered before getting into bed.

She hadn't expected to be able to sleep, knowing that

a raid was imminent, but the combination of alcohol and heavy dancing had worn her out. She drifted off within minutes of lying down, and was awakened suddenly at two AM by the sound of pounding on her door.

Terrified, both by the knowledge of what was about to happen and the noise of someone pounding on the door while she was barely half awake, she climbed out of bed and pulled the door open. She was instantly grabbed and thrown back onto the bed, where she was held down by one man as two more begin ransacking the room.

It took them only a couple of minutes to dig through the dresser drawers, and then they started on her suitcases. Seconds later, one of the men shouted as he held up the envelope of drugs. The man holding Sarah down suddenly yanked her to her feet and began shouting in her face, but she didn't understand anything he was saying.

The blank look on her face told him she didn't understand, so he grabbed the envelope from the other man, shook it in front of her face and shouted, "*Yaba!*"

A few more shouted words, even though she didn't understand them, surely telling her she was under arrest. Without even trying, she began to cry and protest, but she was spun around and handcuffed, then dragged out the door and to the elevator. A few people in the lobby stared as she was obviously led to a police car waiting just outside the front door.

At the local police station, Sarah was shoved into a holding cell with a dozen other people, both male and female. Several of them were intoxicated, and she had to fight off advances more than once, but she managed to hold her own. For the next seven hours, she sat in the cell and watched as one by one, the others were led out and seated at various desks in the room outside.

When her turn came, she was shoved into a seat beside the desk of a large, ugly-looking man. He typed into a computer for a few moments, then looked up at her.

"You American?"

Sarah swallowed and nodded. "Yes, I'm an American. I need to talk to somebody from our embassy, can you call them for me?"

"Maybe later," the big man said. "Right now I tell you you under arrest for sell *yaba*. Why you think you come here and sell drug?"

"Selling? But I wasn't selling anything," she protested. "I just thought—somebody offered to sell me some, and I hadn't ever tried it so I thought I'd see what it was like. I just bought a little bit for me, I wasn't going to sell it to anyone."

"You got twelve pills," the man said. "Too many for you. Only reason you have so many is to sell. I charge you with possession for sale, very serious here in Thailand. You get five years, maybe ten, maybe more. We no like Americans come here to sell drugs. Very bad, very bad."

"But I—"

The man waved a hand to shush her, and she fell silent. He typed on his computer keyboard for several minutes, then looked up at her again. "What you name?"

Sarah had used the intervening minutes to get herself under control and remind herself that this was all part of the mission. "Kayla," she said. "Kayla Maguire."

A dozen more questions demanded her home address and other information, all of which she provided from the manufactured mission identity. If anyone bothered to check, they would find that Kayla Maguire had lived at the provided address for almost a year, and actually worked where she claimed to. Such records are easy to manufacture for an organization like E & E, and Donald Jefferson had taken pains to make them as realistic as possible.

By the time the questioning was done, it was nearly noon. Sarah was pushed back into the holding cell and given a small bowl of rice and fish to eat. No sooner did she have it, however, than another prisoner snatched the bowl from her hands and began shoveling it into his own mouth. Sarah didn't even bother to protest, knowing it would be futile.

Two hours later, she was taken out once more, handcuffed again and led through several hallways into a small courtroom. She was pushed into a chair at the table, and the man sitting beside her looked at her for only a second before standing up to address the judge.

Sarah couldn't understand anything that was said, but she knew it wasn't good. When the man beside her sat once more, he turned to her and said, "You guilty. Police find drugs, you all alone, you guilty. You plead guilty, you get smaller sentence, only three years. You no plead guilty, you get twenty-five years."

Sarah stared at him in disbelief, which she didn't have to fake. No wonder there were so many Americans in Thai prisons, she thought. Almost anyone would take a plea bargain like that, knowing there was no hope of any viable defense. She let the tears flow that were already hovering behind her eyelids, bit her bottom lip and nodded.

A man stood once more and spoke to the judge in rapid Thai, after which the judge nodded and replied. Something was scribbled on a piece of paper that was passed to the judge, who signed it. A clerk took the paper and left the room for a couple of minutes, then came back and handed a copy to the man that Sarah assumed was her attorney.

He looked at her again. "You smart girl," he said. "Judge only give you three years. Sentence start today, you go to prison tomorrow."

"But," Sarah protested, "just like that? I thought this was just like an arraignment or something."

"This how we do things," the man said. "You Westerns, judge don't waste time. You plead guilty, he give you sentence right now."

"But, can't I talk to…"

"Someone from American Embassy come see you in prison," the man said. "Maybe this week, maybe next week."

A hand grasped her by her upper arm and she was pulled up out of the chair and whisked out the door. She thought she was being taken back to the holding cell, but the guard escorting her took another turn and she was led into a different section of the building. In this one, female prisoners sat in individual cells, and Sarah was pushed into the first empty one they came to.

The guard removed her handcuffs and pointed at the bunk, obviously telling her to sit. She did, and the door was slammed shut and locked. She leaned back against the steel wall behind the bunk and stared around herself.

She could see into the cells across from her, and noticed a couple of Caucasian women. "Hey," she called out. "Are you Americans?"

One of them ignored her completely, but the other looked over at her and grinned. "Nah, mate," she said. "We're from Australia. They get you for *yaba?*"

Sarah nodded. "Yeah. I bought a little bit last night, just

to try it, and the next thing I know I've got cops busting in my hotel room door."

The woman laughed. "Yeah, it's an old game," she said. "Some of the dealers, they make double money by selling drugs to *farangs* and then takin' the piss on us. They tell the cops they sell to, probably get twice as much money as they did off you. That's how we got here, too. What hotel you staying in?"

"The Dream Hotel," Sarah said. "I only bought twelve pills, they said that was too much."

"Yeah," the woman said, nodding. "Two or three, they call that recreational, but any more than that and you must be a drug dealer. You did a plea, right? Got a short time?"

"The lawyer said I'd get like twenty years if I didn't," Sarah replied, "so, yeah, I did. Was that a mistake?"

"Ha!" the woman barked. "Twenty woulda been light if you hadn't. More likely you'd've got life! They like giving life to us *farangs,* sweets! Be glad you was smart, and you better hope you got fam back home what'll send you money for food and stuff."

Sarah knew what she was saying, but let her face register surprise to stay in character. "They have to send me money to buy food? What if you don't have any money?"

"Then you can work for one of the women who does, or you can put out to the Toms. Toms is the lezzies, they'd love to get onto a pretty little sheila like you! You won't go hungry, no worries!"

Sarah leaned back as if the woman's words had disturbed her, and said nothing more. A few minutes later, another guard came and got her, took her to a shower room and made her change into jailhouse clothing: a pair of midcalf pants, a loose pullover shirt and what seemed a female version of boxer underwear, but no bra. Sarah understood what was happening, even if she didn't understand anything the woman said to her, and a half-hour later she was back in the same cell.

The Australian women were gone, and different women were in their cell. Sarah wondered where they'd gone, but didn't ask.

Sometime later, she was given another bowl of rice and fish. Since there was no one to steal it from her, she actually got to eat it, and then lay back on her bunk. She was genuinely tired, after getting very little rest the night before, and sleep claimed her long before the lights went out at ten.

ELEVEN

W hile Sarah was enduring her ordeal, Noah and the other men were staying in character. Thursday meant another day of visiting inmates and talking with prison staff, though the warden still declined to give any kind of interview.

They had visited two women, one American and an Australian, and then visited with a man from the UK. After each visit, they had gone to the visitors' store and purchased gifts for them, usually food and toiletries. The British man had asked them to send him books if they could, and they managed to find a few American spy novels in the store for him.

When their day ended, they went back to their hotel and waited for darkness to fall. Noah had decided to go ahead and cut their entrance that night, but instead of all three of them climbing the wall, Marco would make that climb and do the job alone. Noah and Neil would keep watch from a safe distance, each of them armed with the special guns they had been provided.

The ferry didn't run that late, so they took a taxi to the area near the prison where they had set out their tracking units. The ride took about an hour, but it was worth it. Not only would no one recall them on the boat, but the taxi driver would only remember dropping them at a restaurant nearby.

Luckily, that section of wall was just as deserted as it had been on the mockup. Marco shot the grapple up the wall, shimmied up it like a spider monkey and was back down on the ground less than forty minutes later. He headed back toward the restaurant without even looking in their direction.

"All set," he said when Noah and Neil rejoined him. They ate a late dinner and then lingered a little longer over some of the local beer before getting another taxi to take them back to the hotel. If everything was going according to plan, Sarah had already been arrested and should be showing up at the prison within the next few days.

On Friday, they selected three more inmates to visit and went about the day just as they had done before. Neil had wanted to carry the tablet along with them, but Noah had vetoed the idea.

"We don't want to run the risk of someone seeing the layout of the prison on its screen," he said. "Leave it in the room, and make sure the tracking software is turned off. The last thing we need is for one of the housekeepers to notice something funny on it. Sarah will be all right for the day if she happens to turn up while we're away."

Neil grumbled but did as he was told. They spent their allotted visits as they had done before, even to the point of wasting time choosing gifts to send to those they had visited. By the time they were ready to head back to their hotel, it was nearly five o'clock.

As soon as they entered the room, Neil grabbed the monitor and turned it on. He activated the tracking software and then made a sour face. "Nothing yet," he said.

"There's no telling how long it will take them to get her sentenced," Noah said. "I'm sure it won't be more than a few days, but I have my doubts they bother on the weekends. Most likely, we won't see her appear before Monday, now."

Neil grimaced and started to set the tablet down, but suddenly it sounded a tone that made him look again. His face broke into a smile as he looked up at Noah.

"Get this," he said, "she just came in range. According to the blip, she's moving along the street we were on last night."

Noah and Marco crowded around him and watched as the blip that indicated her presence moved along the street and came to a stop in front of the main entrance. A moment later it moved slowly inside, and toward the women's section.

"Perfect timing," Noah said. "At least now we have something to keep us busy through the weekend."

* * *

The day had seemed excessively long to Sarah, as she waited for someone to come and take her to the prison. The sheer boredom of sitting in a cell with nothing to do was driving her crazy, and every minute that passed without anyone calling her out of it seemed to last an hour or more.

She had been awakened with another bowl of rice, minus the fish, for breakfast. She had eaten it in the interest of keeping up her strength, then sat for what she thought must have been six hours before another bowl was brought for her lunch. The other inmates close to her did not speak English, so she didn't bother trying to talk with them. That increased her level of boredom and frustration, as more hours passed.

She had just reached the point of deciding it was time to scream for attention when a third bowl of rice, this time with chunks of chicken, was shoved through the bars at her. She tried to ask the guard what time it was, but the woman simply shrugged and walked away. Like Noah, Sarah decided that she probably wouldn't be moving until Monday, and sat down forlornly on her bunk to eat. The thought of two more days of such intense boredom was more intimidating than the thought of entering the prison itself.

She had just finished eating and set her bowl outside her cell when she heard keys rattle and a guard stepped up to open her door. "Come on," the Thai woman said. "You go prison now."

Sarah tried not to let the relief show on her face, certain that staying in character would require her to look frightened, but the woman paid no attention. She was told to turn around in the doorway and her hands were cuffed behind her back, then a hand grabbed her arm and marched her out and down the hallway once again.

This time, she was led out a door and directly into a van that held six other women. None of them had been in her cellblock, but she noticed a couple of Caucasians in the mix.

"Hey," she said to one of them. "Any idea what's going on?"

"Yeah, baby," the woman said. "We're going off to the Bangkok Hilton. How long you get?"

Sarah grimaced. "Three years," she said. "I was stupid and bought some of those *yaba* pills. I just wanted to try, I never had a chance before."

"Yeah, me too." Sarah noticed that her accent seemed

American. "These idiots said I was trying to sell it, can you believe that?"

"They said that about me, too," Sarah said. "I only had twelve pills, is that really so much?"

"Twelve? Hell, I had fifty. I scored it for me and my friends, but they got me before I even got back to my hotel room. Somebody snitched me out."

Sarah nodded. "Me, too," she said. "From what I understand, the dealers like to sell it to us and then tell the cops who they sold it to. I guess they get paid for ratting us out."

A guard stepped into the van and started shouting, and Sarah didn't need an interpreter to know she was being told to shut up. She sat back in her seat and stayed quiet as the van moved out.

The ride lasted about an hour and a half, and very few of the women tried to talk during the journey. Sarah simply looked out the window beside her at the passing scenery, but her mind was racing as she uttered silent prayers that Noah was on station and ready for her arrival at the prison. With any luck, she would find Sharon Ingersoll quickly and this whole nightmare could come to an end.

The van arrived at the prison and the women were let off one at a time. Female guards from the prison had come out to escort them in individually, and it was nearly 20 minutes before it was Sarah's turn to get out. She made a point of not giving the guard any resistance, and was quickly brought into a room where she was seated at a desk.

A pretty young woman was sitting there and she looked up and smiled at Sarah. The guard handed a large envelope to the woman, and she opened it swiftly to dump out its contents onto her desk.

Sarah was surprised to see not only the paperwork regarding her case, but a substantial amount of Thai currency. Apparently, the money she had had in her hotel room had been correctly counted and sent along with her. The young woman at the desk counted through it, then looked up at Sarah.

"You are Kay-la Mag-wire?" Despite being a native, her accent sounded British.

"Yes," Sarah said.

"Okay, you have 18,400 baht. I put it in your account, so you can use it to buy what you need. Be careful with it, and it will last you a long time in here." The woman shoved the money into an envelope, sealed it and put it in a drawer of her desk, then turned to a computer and began entering the information from Sarah's paperwork. A moment later, another printer spat out a strip of paper. The woman slid it into a plastic sleeve and then used a tool to affix it to Sarah's wrist. "My name is Nan," she said as she did so. "I see many American girls like you come into this place. You have only three years, that is not long. If you be very careful, you will not have any trouble in here."

The simple human kindness in her voice was more than Sarah could handle, and tears began to flow down her cheeks. "Thank you," she said. "I plan to be very, very careful."

Nan nodded her head. "Are you all alone? Do you know anyone who is in our prison?"

For a brief moment, Sarah thought about asking about Sharon Ingersoll, but common sense prevailed and she only shook her head. "No," she said. "This is my first trip to Thailand, and I don't know anybody here. My lawyer said someone from the embassy will come to see me here?"

Once again, Nan nodded. "Yes, they will come, but it may not be soon. There is only one man who comes for the American women, and he is very busy. I think it may be two or three weeks before he comes again, and he will have many of you to see. You may not see him that time, but he will come and talk to you when he can. His name is Jonathan, but that is all I know."

Sarah managed to stop the sniffles. "Thank you. You speak very good English."

"I went to school in London," Nan said. "Sometimes I wish I had stayed there, but I take care of my mother, so I had to come back. I was lucky to get a good job like this." She tapped a series of keys on her computer and a couple of papers shot out of a printer nearby. "You're all done," she said.

Nan waved a hand in the air and the guard took hold of Sarah by the arm once again. She was led into a holding cell, just like the one she had been placed in the mockup the first day of their practice runs. Some of the other women from the van were already sitting there, but guards were taking them out one at a time and leading them into the prison itself.

She was led into another shower room, where she went through the same routine she had experienced in the mockup. The prison clothes they gave her were only slightly different from the ones she had been given in the jail, which were tossed into a box, but at least the boxers were replaced by a pair of cotton panties. Since it was already late in the day, she was led directly to a sleeping room and pushed inside.

Sarah stood just inside the entrance and scanned for an empty pallet, but let her eyes rove over the women in the room at the same time. There were a few Caucasians, but none of them looked like the photo she had been shown of Sharon Ingersoll.

A woman on a pallet near the door tapped her on the foot and pointed across the room. Sarah looked where the woman indicated and saw an empty pallet, then carefully stepped over and around the women between her and her goal. When she reached it, she sat down and looked at her neighbors.

One of them was a black woman, and she looked at Sarah questioningly. "American?" she asked.

"Yeah," Sarah said. "You?"

"Yep. I'm Raylene, from Birmingham. Where you from?"

"Muncie, Indiana. Have you been here very long?"

"Starting my fourth year," Raylene said. "You got family to help you with money?"

Sarah thought quickly and decided she didn't want to mention that she had money on the books already, so she nodded. "Yeah, a little bit. Do I really have to buy my own food?"

"Honey, you got to pay for it somehow. Did you have any money when you come in?"

"Not much," Sarah said. "I'll need to write home as soon as possible and get my folks to send me more as soon as they can."

The woman smiled and let her eyes roam over Sarah's body. "Well, don't you worry none, honey. If it takes a little while, Raylene will take care of you, don't you sweat it."

The look on Raylene's face was enough to tell Sarah what the woman was proposing, but she thought it best to pretend ignorance. "Oh, thanks," she said, "but I should be okay until I get hold of them."

Another woman, this one apparently British, waved a hand to get Sarah's attention. "Don't you get mixed up with Raylene," the woman said loudly. "She won't do anything for anyone without there being something in it for her. The last thing you want to do in this place is owe anybody any favors, take my word for that."

Raylene glared at the woman, but didn't say anything. Sarah glanced back and forth between the two of them, then lay down on her pallet and folded her hands under her head.

Dear Lord, she prayed silently, *please let me find Sharon right away and then let Noah get us out of here. Please, Lord, I don't know how long I can take this place.*

TWELVE

Neil got onto his computer first thing Saturday morning and started looking at inmates they could visit for the day. "Hey, Noah?"

"Yeah?" Noah said.

The skinny kid grinned at him. "How about Sharon Ingersoll? She's on the list."

Noah shook his head. "I don't want any association between us. If she got a visit from some random Americans just before she apparently escapes, I think it would set off alarm bells that would piss off the Dragon Lady. Let's stick to men today."

"You got it," Neil said. He chose three male inmates: one American, one Brazilian and one from New Zealand. He printed out the bio sheets on all three and passed them to his boss.

Noah scanned over each one, passing it to Marco as he finished. He was just finishing the last one when Marco grunted. "Something wrong with that one?" he asked.

"The Brazilian guy," Marco said. "Juergen Klug. Sounds more like a German."

"World War II," Noah said. "Toward the end, a lot of Nazi personnel began jumping ship and heading for South America. Argentina and Brazil were considered

German allies for a while, so a lot of them settled there."

Marco nodded. "Yeah, I remember my history lessons. Just struck me as odd."

"You're odd," Neil said.

"I think we all are," Noah added in. "Let's go get some breakfast and then go play reporter."

"One minute," Neil replied. "Just want to check on our girl." He picked up the tablet and turned it on, then held it out toward Noah. The blip showed her in one of the workrooms. "Looks like they've given her a work assignment already."

"Good. The more she gets to mingle with the other inmates, the quicker she's going to locate the target, and the sooner we can get her out of there."

Neil cocked an eyebrow at him. "Do I detect a hint of worry?"

Noah shrugged. "I'm not worried," he said, "I'm just quite certain she wants to get out of there as soon as possible."

"Noah, I can set this up so that the display is turned off, but it will sound a tone if she signals us. Want me to bring it along?"

"No. The plan is to go in during the midnight shift change. She won't send a signal during the day, and we'll be close to our entry point shortly before midnight, every night from now until she does."

"Okay. I'll just leave it on the charger, then."

They left the hotel and went to a nearby restaurant for breakfast, then made their way toward the ferry landing. The boat seemed unusually crowded that morning, but Noah figured it was simply because of the weekend visiting opportunities. The number of women with children bore out that theory.

A different clerk was working the registration desk, so they had to go through the entire process of showing identification and explaining the reason for their visits once again. By the time they got the clerk to approve them, it was already close to eleven.

* * *

Sarah was roused before the sun came up and led with the rest of her bunkmates to the feeding room, where tables were laid out. Bowls sat on all of the tables, but most of the women shoved the bowls aside and sat down to eat the food they were pulling out of pockets and from inside their clothing. Those who didn't seem to have any food either ate from the bowls or begged from the women close to them.

Sarah sat down and looked at the bowl in front of her, then cringed back away from it. It contained rice, but there were a number of insects in the bowl, as well. The woman across from her, a scarred and gray-haired woman with a French accent, leaned forward and pointed at the bowl.

"If you have no money," she said, "this is for you. You get one bowl with rice, and don't let them catch you trying to eat any extra. The guards get very angry if you try." She used her plastic spoon to flick a couple of bugs out of her own bowl.

Sarah shook her head. "It has bugs in it," she said. "I've got some money on my account, when do I get to buy food?"

The French woman looked at her, her eyes going wide. "You can buy food when the cart comes this morning. Is there anything you need that I can do, so you might buy me some food?" Sarah could sense the desperation in her voice, and knew that she could probably ask anything at that moment.

The pitiful tone in her voice touched a soft spot in Sarah's heart. "I don't have a lot of money," she said cautiously, "but I can help you out a little bit. But the only thing I need is—I heard about another American girl here, Sharon Ingersoll. Would you happen to know her?"

The woman's eyes went wide for a moment. "Sharon? Yes, she works with me in sewing room." She looked around. "But she sleeps in another room, and her room will be next to come in here." She turned back to Sarah. "I am Jacqueline," she said. "If you stay close to me, I will show you which one is Sharon. And you will buy me some food?"

Sarah smiled. "Jacqueline, I'll be happy to," she said. "Just stick with me until we get the chance."

The two of them sat and talked for a few minutes, and Sarah noticed that Jacqueline pushed her rice bowl away, even though she'd only taken a couple of bites. Obviously, the prospect of getting some decent food was more appealing than the demands of hunger.

Sarah learned that Jacqueline was serving a twenty-year sentence for selling drugs. She had actually been caught in the act of selling *yaba*, which was why her sentence was so much more severe, but her attitude was good. She blamed only herself for the situation she was in, and was looking forward to completing her eighth year in a few months. After that, the French government would have her transferred to a prison in her own country, which would result in her immediate parole.

It was at that point that they heard the sounds of new inmates entering the room, and those sitting at the tables began to leave. Jacqueline turned in her seat and watched the door for a moment, then broke into a smile and pointed. "That is her," she said.

Sarah looked at the woman she indicated and it was all she could do to keep the relief from showing on her face. This was definitely Sharon Ingersoll, and Sarah was struck by the thought that she was one of those young women who looked beautiful no matter what.

"Just a moment," Jacqueline said. "I will bring her over here." She rose from her seat and hurried over to Sharon, and Sarah saw her pointing back at herself. A moment later, the two of them came and sat at the tables. Sharon glanced at the bowl of rice that Sarah had pushed away, but then she raised her eyes and looked Sarah over.

"Jackie said you wanted to talk to me?" Sharon asked.

"Yes," Sarah said. "I'm Kayla. I heard about you last night, another American girl. You're not going to eat that rice, are you? That's the bowl I pushed away when I got here."

"They don't bring up fresh ones," Sharon said. "That bowl was most likely sitting there for a couple of hours before you got to it." She shrugged her shoulders. "Gotta eat something."

"If you can hold out till the food cart comes, I'll buy you some good stuff. I've got a little money."

Sharon looked at her suspiciously. "Yeah? And what's it going to cost me?"

"Not a thing," Sarah said. "I don't speak the local language at all, so I want a friend who's American, like me. No strings attached, I promise you."

Sharon looked into her eyes for a long moment, then slowly pushed the bowl away again. "Okay," she said, "as long as you understand I'm not into girls."

Sarah laughed. "No problem," she said, "neither am I." She glanced over at Jacqueline. "Any idea when the food cart comes?"

"In about an hour," Sharon said. "Mostly they sell fruits and vegetables, but they do have little packages of tuna and sardines, and some little things they call cookies."

Sarah nodded. "Okay," she said, "I can probably get us each enough for a week or so."

Jacqueline shook her head. "Do not buy so much," she said. "Only buy enough for each day, or the others will steal it. Some of the Toms can get to the lockers in the night, and they will take any food they find. Only buy what you can carry each day."

Sharon nodded her agreement. "She's right. If you set something down or put it in your locker, it will be gone before you know it. You only want to get enough to get you through the day."

"So the cart comes every morning?"

"Yeah, about the same time. We'll have to get in line as soon as we see it, or we might end up waiting an hour or more while they refill it."

"Okay. Where does it show up? Maybe we can get in position before too many others do."

A guard walked toward their table, eyeing Sarah and Jacqueline. The Frenchwoman tapped Sarah on the arm. "We should go now," she said. "We are not supposed to stay here after our room has finished eating." She looked at Sharon. "You come with us now, yes?"

The three of them rose from the table and walked out the door, and Jacqueline led the way to a day room that had several televisions and numerous tables where women were playing games. "The cart will come here," she said. "After we get done with the cart, we must go to work. Do you have a job yet?"

"No. Will they assign me one today?"

Sharon grinned. "You can assign yourself," she said. "We both work in sewing, just come with us and the room boss will put you to work. Where are you sleeping?"

Sarah shrugged. "Last night, they put me in the room Jacqueline is in. Do I have to stay there?"

"No," Jacqueline said. "We can go to any room to sleep, as long as we get there in time to find an empty pallet to sleep on. They count three times every night to make sure we all here, but as long as the numbers add up they do not really care where we are. We can all go to one room tonight. We just need to go early, before they tell everyone to go to bed. That way, we can find maybe some beds together."

"Okay, good," Sarah said, though she worried a bit about how to talk to Sharon alone. She decided to play it by ear and watch for an opportunity.

It was almost another hour before the food cart appeared, but Jacqueline had managed to get them close to the front of the line. Sarah let the other two choose the items they would buy, then they helped her to sign for them, using the inmate number on her bracelet. They shoved the oranges, bananas, carrots and cookies into their pockets, and then Sarah followed the other two toward the sewing room.

As Sharon had predicted, the woman running the sewing room simply told Sarah to start carrying bolts of cloth to where other women were cutting it into parts for pants and shirts. They worked steadily for about three hours, and then Jacqueline told Sarah it was lunchtime, but rather than returning to the room where they'd had break-fast, Jacqueline and Sharon led her down a hallway to a smaller room. A few women sat on the floor, there, and they each took a spot and did likewise, leaning against the wall.

They each ate some of the fruits and vegetables they had bought, careful to make sure they left enough for dinner. The lunch break lasted half an hour, and the two women told Sarah more about the prison and how it worked until it was time to go back to their jobs.

During the afternoon, the room boss sent Jacqueline after more cloth and thread, and Sarah decided to take a chance on trying to talk to Sharon. She waited until the two of them were in a corner together—Sharon was doing the kind of sorting that Sarah had done in their practice sessions—then glanced around to make sure no one could overhear.

"I need to talk to you about something," she whispered. "But you have to trust me and not tell anyone what I'm about to say."

Sharon looked at her suspiciously. "What is it?"

"Sharon," she began softly, "I'm not who I claim to be. I work for the United States government, same as you. I'm part of a secret rescue mission to get you out of here."

Sharon's eyebrows rose slightly. "I was actually won-dering about that," she whispered back. "Somebody told me someone was coming, but I didn't know whether to believe them or not. Are you serious?"

"Yes. The rest of my team is waiting for me to signal them that I found you, and then they'll come and grab us out of here. We have to be sure that we're sleeping in the same room, because they'll come in during the midnight shift change."

Sharon stared at her for a few seconds, then composed herself and went back to sorting the clothes. "Okay," she said. "What about Jacqueline?"

"She's not part of this, and can't know anything about it until it's too late. Besides, she's about to get out of here legally. You and I will have new identities to help us get out of the country once this is over. If she escapes now, it would probably ruin her life."

"Okay, I won't say anything. How long, do you think? Before we get out, I mean."

"I can't be sure," Sarah replied. "It's possible it could even be tonight, as long as we're together when the shift changes. Is there any way you can know when it's about to happen?"

Sharon nodded. "Yes, they lock our doors about ten or fifteen minutes beforehand. The locks are loud, so it's obvious."

Sarah grinned. "That's what our intelligence said, but I wanted to be sure. Okay, as soon as we hear that lock, I can signal my team. About ten minutes later, they'll be in here to get us. They're going to give you a piece of gum, and you've got to put it in your mouth and start chewing as fast as you can. They have some special little guns that shoot out a drug that just sort of turns off the brain. The gum is an antidote, so it won't affect you if it hits you. Chewing it gets the antidote into your bloodstream in a hurry, so chew it fast. I'm going to get back to work so nobody notices us talking." She walked away and began carrying cloth again.

Jacqueline returned a bit later, and they continued working through the afternoon. It was getting close to six by the time their shift ended, and they went back to the room where they had breakfast to eat their dinner.

Sharon acted normal, and Jacqueline seemed none the wiser. When they finished eating, they went to the day room and played a game of spades with some badly battered cards until it was getting close to bedtime.

Jacqueline stacked the cards and rose from her chair. "They will call bedtime in just a little while," she said. "We should go now and find a place to stay together." Sarah and Sharon also rose and followed her out the door. She stopped at the first sleeping room and pointed inside, indicating that it was nearly empty. They were able to take pallets that were just inside the door, and Sarah began to feel excited. If all went well, she knew, she'd be back with Noah before morning.

THIRTEEN

"Heads up," Neil said at just past 9:30 that night. "She just settled down into a sleeping room. Think she might have found the target yet?"

"No way to tell," Noah said. "All we can do is be close to our entry point and ready to move if she sends the signal. Let's head out now, I want to be in position long before the shift change begins."

With the special guns slung under their arms and covered by light jackets, and the second grapple launcher stuffed down Marco's pants, they left the hotel and caught a taxi. It took them to the restaurant where they'd had dinner after cutting their entryway, and they went inside to order a snack while they waited. The restaurant was open until midnight, so they were able to sit there and sip coffee after they finished eating.

At 11:30, they left the restaurant and began strolling around near the wall they would have to scale. There was no one else around, so after a few minutes of surveillance they slipped behind some bushes close to the wall. Neil carried the tablet and activated the program that would tell him when Sarah snapped the panic button.

Noah had his phone in his hand, ready to tell Darrell

Knapp to drop the body into the alley as soon as they got that signal.

* * *

By the time the men had left the restaurant, Jacqueline had already drifted off to sleep. Sarah and Sharon were lying on their pallets side-by-side, so close that they were actually pressed against each other, but both of them were wide awake. Sarah had one hand inside her shirt, waiting for the sound of the lock. Her nerves were jangling, and she was whispering silent prayers that the rescue would come off without any problems.

Suddenly, there were voices in the hallway, and Sharon looked toward the door in surprise. Some of the voices were male, a surprise since she'd been told it was very rare for men to appear in the women's prisons. They were speaking in Thai, so neither of them could understand what was being said, but the looks on the faces of some of the other inmates made them nervous.

Jacqueline was roused by the chatter and raised up on one elbow. She listened for a moment, then looked at the other two. "It is the snatch," she said. "It's happened a few times before since I have been here. Some men, they are pimps, they pay the night guards to let them take a few of the pretty ones."

Sarah's eyes went wide. "Are you serious?"

"*Oui,* yes," Jacqueline said. "Lie down and hide your faces. Sometimes they take Western girls."

A light was suddenly shined through the bars of the door, striking the three of them full in the face. Sarah and Sharon ducked quickly, holding their breaths as the door was flung open. A rough hand grabbed Sharon's hair and yanked her up, and the light was shined on her face again.

She panicked. "Kayla, help me!"

Sarah reacted without thinking, rising to a kneeling position and staring at the man who was dragging Sharon to her feet. "Hey!" she yelled, and the light was turned on her.

A second man laughed and reached for Sarah's hair. Like Sharon, she was jerked cruelly to her feet and dragged out the door as Jacqueline stared on in shock.

Thinking quickly and praying it would do some good, Sarah pressed her hand to her ribs and felt for the panic button. She pressed hard on it a couple of times, and felt a sudden twinge as it snapped. *Oh, God,* she thought, *please let Noah see that I'm moving in the wrong direction! Please, let him get the message that something is wrong!*

Once they were in the hallway, both girls' arms were wrenched behind their backs and their wrists quickly secured with zip ties. Hands grabbed their upper arms and they were pushed roughly forward. Sarah started shouting at her captor, but a hand smacked the back of her head and she didn't need an interpreter to know she had been told to shut up. With the guards paying no attention to what was happening, she had no choice but to comply.

Moments later, they were hustled out the front door and pushed into the back of a van. Four other young women were already there, all of them Asian. The doors were slammed shut and they were in darkness.

"Is this it?" Sharon asked. "Is this part of the rescue?"

Sarah turned toward the sound of her voice but could not see her. "I don't think so," she said.

* * *

"She's moving," Neil said. "Not sure why, but she just came out of the sleeping room and—Bingo! There it is, we got the signal."

"That's good," Noah said, "but where is she going? Once she sends the signal, she's supposed to stay put with the target."

"No idea. She's still moving, though, headed toward the front of the prison, up by the intake office. Still moving, same direction—What the..." Neil said. "Noah, something's wrong. According to the monitor, Sarah just walked out the front door!" He held the tablet out to show Noah.

Noah looked at the monitor, noting that the blip indicating Sarah's position suddenly started moving rapidly down the road outside the prison and would pass their position in only seconds. He looked up to see the lights of a vehicle, but there was no time to take any action. A van drove past them, and another glance at the monitor confirmed that Sarah had to be inside.

Noah broke into a run with both of the other men right on his heels, but the van was already moving at more than forty miles-per-hour. It was out of sight within seconds, and the blip vanished from the monitor at the same time.

"Holy crap," Neil said, "do you think her cover was blown?"

Noah shook his head. "No idea." He looked around behind them and saw no sign of any activity from the prison, so he lifted the phone and pushed the call button to contact Knapp.

"Wong Ho's Pizza," Knapp answered. "Can I take your order?"

"Camelot," Noah said. "There's been a situation. Abort the drop. I need immediate pickup."

There was a split second's hesitation, and then Knapp

came back on the line. "We see you. Be there in ten seconds."

Headlights came on in an alley to their left and a van pulled up beside them. Side doors opened and let Noah and his men climb inside. A short Asian man was driving, with Knapp in the front passenger seat. He was facing toward the back. "What's going on?"

"My operative was just taken out of the prison," Noah said. "She was in the van that just went down this road. Any idea what this could mean?"

Knapp looked at the driver and an expression of dismay crossed his face. The driver shrugged, and he turned back to Noah. "Question," he said. "Is she a really pretty girl?"

"Yes," Noah said. "Why?"

"Oh, Geez," Knapp said. "Listen, about once or twice a year, a few girls go missing out of the prison. They're always the exceptionally pretty ones, some of them downright beautiful. Local authorities deny it ever happens, and those women just disappear off the face of the earth. You've heard about the Thai sex trade? Well, we're pretty sure that's what happens to them."

Noah's blank, emotionless expression seemed to unnerve Knapp. "Are you telling me that she may have been taken by sex slavers, and it's all a big coincidence?"

Knapp spread his hands wide, shaking his head. "Look, I know how that sounds, but that's all it can be. None of our intelligence services have ever been able to break these people, we have no idea when they're going to strike or where they disappear to. I can start calling everybody in the local intelligence community, but odds on this is going to be a shock to them, too."

"Then get started," Noah said. He lifted his own phone

and punched a speed dial icon.

"Thank you for calling Brigadoon Investments," came a recorded voice. "I'm afraid no one is in the office today. If you know your party's extension, you may enter it at any time to leave a message. To leave a general message, please dial zero."

Noah punched in 9904, and a new voice answered instantly. "This is Ops."

"This is Camelot. I have a situation."

"One moment." There was a series of beeps on the line, and Allison Peterson's voice said, "Camelot? What's going on?"

"Sarah was just removed from the prison," Noah said. "Immediately after signaling us that she had found the target, she was taken away in a van, possibly by members of the Asian sex trade. I was not able to follow and have no idea where she's being taken."

"Good God," Allison said, "how many times is that girl going to be abducted? What about the target?"

"I have no knowledge about the target."

There was silence on the line for all of ten seconds. "Camelot, acquiring the target is the mission priority, but with the original plan in ruins, we're going to have to do it the hard way. Team Cinderella happens to be in Hanoi, that's only a couple of hours away from you. Their mission is already complete, so I'm going to divert them to Bangkok. They'll make contact with you in the morning, your time. In the meanwhile, I'll make certain the target is still in the prison. She is every bit as attractive as Sarah, so if the sex slavers took her and they were together, it's possible both were taken. If that's happened your entire mission will change, but if she's still there, you have to devise a new plan for getting her out. I'll call you as soon as I know something."

"Yes, Ma'am," Noah said. "May I put our people here to work on trying to find out where they might have taken her?"

"Absolutely. And if you do, I'll authorize any actions necessary to retrieve her, *after* you complete your mission. Just remember that the mission comes first."

"Understood." Noah ended the call and turned to Knapp. "I want you to use every contact you've got," he said, "or do anything else you have to do, but I want to know where she's gone. You know how to reach me if you learn anything, right?"

"Yep," Knapp said. "I've got your number. Can we drop you guys somewhere?"

Noah glanced around at the body that was strapped to a gurney in the back of the van, connected to beeping machines that were keeping it just barely alive. "Yes," he said. "The closest possible place to get a taxi."

"You got it." The driver put the van in gear and drove sedately along until they came to a brightly lit area full of go-go bars. "You'll find plenty of them around here," Knapp said. "I'll be in touch as soon as I know anything."

The three men climbed out of the van and it drove away quickly. Marco pointed toward a taxi, and they crossed the street to climb into it. The driver started to object when Noah got into the front seat, but the handful of money Noah held out to him changed his complaint into a smile.

"Okay, okay," the driver said. "Where you wanna go?"

Noah had them driven directly back to the hotel, and the three of them went up to the room. Neither Marco nor Neil had spoken since Sarah's disappearance, but when they got inside, Noah turned and looked at Neil.

The tall, skinny kid had tearstains on his cheeks. "Noah," he said, choking, "we gotta find her."

Noah looked him in the eye. "We will," he said. "Don't worry about that. For now, we all need to get some sleep. There's no telling when we'll get another chance."

Marco looked at him but said nothing, and all three of them took off their shoes and lay back on their beds. Noah was asleep within minutes, but the other two lay there for more than an hour before they managed to relax.

Noah was awakened by the ringing of his phone at four AM, and he had it to his ear instantly. "Camelot," he said.

"It's me," Allison said. "I'm afraid the situation just got worse. The State Department has confirmed that both Kayla Maguire and Sharon Ingersoll are listed as missing from the prison and are presumed to have escaped earlier last night."

"Escaped? According to our people here, these girls usually just disappear and the prison denies knowing anything about it."

"Yeah, they tried that," Allison said dryly. "I guess it took a little pressure from State to get them to own up. Of course, they're never going to admit the truth, but at least we know that both of them are gone and presumably together."

Noah nodded into the phone. "Do any of our intelligence services have any idea where these girls might be taken?"

"Nothing concrete. It seems that they're usually taken somewhere for 'training,' before they find themselves in one of the brothels. You can translate training to mean breaking, tearing them down so that they'll do what they're told. We don't have any solid Intel on where that might be, but CIA has picked up rumors of training grounds scattered all over that part of the world. I'll let you know if I get any information on where any of them might be, but if you come across any intelligence on your own, don't hesitate to act. The target is still top priority, but there's at least a good possibility you can find them both at the same time."

"Understood. Team Cinderella?"

"They are in the air as we speak, and will land at Bangkok airport in about an hour. I've got a car waiting for them so they can come straight to your hotel, and Jenny came up with a good suggestion. Our people there in Bangkok are going to meet her at the airport and provide her with identification naming her as Lisa Maguire. It may come in handy for her to be able to pose as Kayla's sister. I told her that she and her team will be under your orders, so use them as you see fit."

"Very good," Noah said. "I'll wait here for their arrival, and then begin looking at options."

The phone went dead and Noah set it back on the nightstand. Marco and Neil were awake, just looking at him.

"Any news?" Neil asked.

"Sarah and the target are both missing from the prison, so they were probably taken together. It's possible they've been taken to a place where women recruited into the sex trade are broken and trained, but we don't know where that might be. Allison is beating all the intelligence bushes and will let us know if she gets anything. Team Cinderella will be here in a couple of hours, and we'll start figuring out what to do."

Marco grinned. "Cinderella? I worked with her before, she's something else. Nice as can be, most of the time, but as cold-blooded as I've ever seen." He inclined his head toward Noah. "Sorry, Chief, but I haven't seen you work yet."

"No problem. I met Jenny once, during the memorial service after the attack on Neverland. She struck me as professional and capable, and that's what I need. What about her team?"

"She's got Jim Marino, Randy Mitchell and Dave Lange. Marino is her computer man, Lange is the driver and Mitchell's the muscle. The one thing I can tell you for sure is that they are absolutely loyal to her. If she told one of them to sacrifice himself in order to accomplish the mission, he wouldn't hesitate."

Noah just looked at him for a long moment. "I would expect the same from my own team," he said.

"And you'd get it," Neil said. "We all knew what we signed on for. It's always the mission first." He squared his shoulders and looked Noah in the eye. "Moose lived up to that."

Noah nodded. "He certainly did."

Marco looked from one to the other. "Yeah, we all know what the job is. Don't worry, Noah, if it comes down to it, I know how to take a bullet."

Neil laughed sarcastically. "Be careful about that," he said. "I already did, once. It sucks."

Marco nodded. "I know," he said. "I was actually in practice runs with Team Oz when we were attacked. They had me set to be the fourth man for an upcoming mission. When all hell broke loose, we rushed to the HQ like everybody else, and I was hit twice. Left leg and right arm."

Neil's face softened slightly. "Okay, I guess you do. And as much as I hate not having Moose with us, I'm glad you made it. You're not as bad as I thought you were."

FOURTEEN

"**W**here are we going?" Sarah asked, but no one answered her. As far as she could tell, none of the other girls in the van spoke English, and the three men in the front couldn't hear them.

Sharon was sitting close to her, their shoulders touching. "This isn't good, is it?" she asked softly.

"Not even a little bit," Sarah said, but then she gave the other girl a wry grin. "But I can tell you this: if anyone can find us, it's my team. Don't give up hope."

"Do you really think there's a chance?"

Sarah shrugged. "I can't say for sure, of course," she said. "The only thing I know for certain is that Noah will never give up. If he got my signal, he's looking for us already."

Sharon turned to face her. Their eyes had adjusted to the minute amount of light in the van, and they could see each other dimly. "Noah?"

"Yeah," Sarah said. "I'm with an agency you probably never heard of, and Noah is my team leader."

"I figured you were CIA," Sharon said. "Was I wrong?"

"Yeah, I'm afraid so. I know you got a pretty high security clearance, but I probably can't tell you much more than I already have. Let's just say that we're the ones the CIA calls on when they need a mess cleaned up."

"Then how did you get stuck trying to rescue me?"

Sarah hesitated for a moment. "It's because of the work you do. Apparently, your bosses feel like they can't get by without you. They went to the State Department, who went to the CIA, who went to the president..."

"Who went to you. Right?"

"Well, to our boss, anyway. We're just one of several teams that work for our boss."

Sharon leaned her head against the wall of the van. "So, somebody decided I was a mess that needed to be cleaned up, right?"

"Not exactly. I'd say it was more a case of you being too valuable for them to risk losing. You wouldn't believe the lengths they went to to get you out."

"You said something about a signal? How did you signal anyone?"

"Little gizmo under the skin over my ribs. If everything had gone according to plan, I would have used it when they locked our door to get ready for the shift change. We ran a number of practice runs in a mockup of the prison that was pretty accurate, and if everything had worked properly we'd be out by now." She glanced toward the men. "When these guys mucked it up, I figured the only thing I could do was try to give Noah a heads up. I sent the signal to tell him I found you, and I'm hoping he was able to track me. I have a little tracker in my arm, but it's got a short range. He might not be able to see where I'm going, now that we left the prison."

Sharon looked at the man who was facing toward them, holding a gun in his hand. "You really think he'll be able to find us?"

"Well, hopefully the intelligence people will have some idea where they might be taking us. He'll find out, and I guarantee you he'll come looking for us." She grinned again. "I'm actually a little jealous," she said. "While he'll do everything he can to get me out, you are his mission priority. And with Noah, the mission always comes first."

Sharon's eyebrows rose. "I get the feeling he's more than just your boss?"

Sarah nodded slowly. "He asked me to marry him," she said, "just before we began this mission. We're going to talk about it more after we get you out, that has to come first. Believe me, we all get it drilled into us: the mission comes first. The mission always comes first."

"It's kinda that way where I work," Sharon said. "It's all about results. Some of the people I work with have made some incredible discoveries, but if they don't fit in with whatever we're supposed to be working on, the brass just doesn't want to hear about it. Oh, they take our data and pass it off to someone else, but we don't get to continue with it. We have to get back to working on whatever assignment they gave us."

Some of the other women were sliding down and trying to make themselves comfortable. "Look at them," Sarah said. "Noah is always telling me that I should rest whenever I get the chance. He says you never know when you might have to go long periods without the opportunity, so don't pass one up when you get it. Maybe now is a good time to take his advice. We should at least try to lay back and rest, so we can be ready whenever he makes his move."

Sharon let out a sigh. "I suppose you're right," she said. She slid down onto the floor of the van and rested her head on her arm. "Wake me up if anything happens, okay?"

Sarah slid down beside her and assumed a similar position facing her. "That's a promise."

Sharon's breathing slowed only a few minutes later as she drifted off to sleep, and Sarah watched her in surprise for several moments. It was hard to believe that anyone could lie down and go to sleep under the circumstances, but she was even more surprised when she herself awoke sometime later.

Light was just beginning to creep into the van from outside, as the sun started to peek over the horizon. It was still dark, but not as dark as it had been. At a guess, she figured it must be somewhere between five and six in the morning. The van was cruising along at a fairly slow pace, and it sounded like gravel under the tires. Even if she could have seen outside, though, she knew she would never have known where she was at. Thailand was an entirely new experience to her.

It had been nearly midnight when she had been taken, she knew, so they had been on the road for at least five-and-a-half hours. As far as she knew, they could be in Thailand or one of several other countries. The way the van was moving, though, she suspected they were getting somewhere close to their destination.

Her theory was borne out a few minutes later when the van came to a stop. The other women who were still sleeping woke up, including Sharon, and the men in the front seats climbed out. A moment later the back doors were opened and all of them were ordered out of the van.

Sarah realized that they were standing at a small dock, and there was a medium-sized boat tied up to it. Across the water, in the distance, she could see what looked like rocks and trees, and wondered if they were taking a short-cut across a lake until she recognized the smell of salt water. It didn't seem like the ocean, but whatever body of water this was must open onto it.

They were pushed toward the boat, and Sarah simply followed the example of the others when they offered no resistance. Trying to fight or run would probably only get her killed, she knew, and she was even more concerned that Sharon would try to help and meet the same fate. As long as they were both alive, there was still at least some chance that Noah would track them down and get them out of whatever nightmare they had fallen into.

She remembered what Jacqueline had said. Could it truly be that, after all she had been through, she was now being forced into sexual slavery? The thought sent chills down her spine, even though it was not nearly as deadly as things she had already faced. Still, she suspected there could be worse fates.

As long as I'm alive, she thought, *there's hope. I know Noah, and he'll never stop looking for me. All I've got to do is survive until he either finds me, or I get the chance to escape and call for help.*

The women were forced to sit down in the bottom of the boat, which was open. Two of the men sat on the gunwales and watched them while the third took the helm at the back of the vessel. The big outboard motor rumbled to life, the lines were cast off, and a moment later the boat began moving away from the dock.

Sitting in the bottom of the boat, Sarah couldn't really see out. It wasn't until a few minutes later that she began to notice trees appearing over the bow, and realized they were approaching a shoreline, maybe even the coast of an island.

The thought of an island scared her even more than she

already was. If they weren't even on the same continent, how would Noah ever find them?

"Is that some kind of island?" Sharon asked, echoing her own thoughts.

Sarah nodded. "Yeah, I think it is."

Sharon shuddered. "Out of the frying pan," she said, "and into the fire. What the hell have we gotten ourselves into?"

Sarah looked closely at her. "You heard what Jacqueline said, and she was probably right. We just have to do whatever it takes to survive. Understand? Can you do that?"

Sharon looked down at her feet for a long moment, then turned her eyes up to Sarah. "It's just—I'm not a prude or—it's not like I'm a virgin or anything, but I've never been a whore. I don't know if I can..."

"You can do whatever you have to do to survive this," Sarah hissed at her. "I told you, Noah will find us, and we're both too important to throw our lives away. I can guarantee you, he's already realized we're gone, so that means he's already talked to our boss. They'll give him any kind of help he wants in order to complete the mission, and completing the mission means bringing you home safe." She forced herself to smile. "Lucky for me, I'm here with you. That means he's got a chance to bring me home safe, as well."

Sharon just looked at her for another moment, then shrugged her shoulders. "So, if they—you know, if they force us—should we just go along with it?"

Sarah's smile slowly faded away. "The way I see it, it won't matter how much we resist. They're going to get the job done, one way or another. Resisting will probably get us hurt, and it might be smarter to keep ourselves in as good condition as we can."

"Yeah," Sharon said. "I guess so. But how do we live with ourselves after?"

Sarah shook her head. "You're not looking at it right," she said. "This isn't something you're doing, it's something that's being done to you. It's not your fault, Sharon. Giving in to it doesn't mean you're guilty of anything, it means you're preserving your strength for when the time comes for us to act. And you never know," Sarah said, her grin sneaking back. "It might even make them relax, and give us a chance to get away on our own. If we can get near a phone, I guarantee I can get hold of Noah within minutes. Just keep yourself together, and keep yourself alive. That's what's got to happen."

One of the men suddenly pointed at Sarah and shouted something she couldn't understand, but the tone told her he wanted her to shut up. She gave Sharon a meaningful look but closed her mouth. The other girl nodded her understanding.

FIFTEEN

W hen Noah awoke again, Neil and Marco were already up, sitting quietly at the table in their room. Neil had the tablet turned on, but of course there was no sign of Sarah on it.

"Almost eight o'clock," Marco said. "I figure Jenny should be here pretty soon."

Noah nodded. "Probably," he said. "After we talk, we'll go find some breakfast."

Neil rolled his eyes. "Geez, Noah, how can you even think about food right now? God only knows if Sarah is even still alive."

Noah turned to face him. "She's alive," he said. "Sarah's not stupid. She'll know we're going to do all we can to find her, so she'll do whatever it takes to keep herself and Ingersoll alive until we do. As for breakfast, we have to keep our own strength up. We can't let ourselves get run down, because we're going to need all of our faculties when we find her."

"Sheesh," Neil said, but then he shut up.

"The boss is right," Marco said. "Don't get me wrong, I like the girl a lot, but the best chance she's got is the three of us and the reinforcements coming our way."

"I know, I know. It just stinks, that's all. Sarah is like

—like my big sister, or something. I can't help worrying about her." He barked an ironic laugh. "Hell, it seems like that's half of what we do."

Marco started to speak, but he was interrupted by the ringing of Noah's phone. Noah snatched it up instantly.

"Camelot," he said.

"Noah, this is Don Jefferson. I've taken over for Allison for the night, and wanted to bring you up to date. Thailand's National Intelligence Agency confirms that the *Nay Thas*—that means 'Slave Masters,' it's what the organizations behind forced prostitution call themselves—maintain what they call training compounds throughout both Thailand and Cambodia, though we have no idea where they might be."

"Understood," Noah said. "I'm assuming I still have authority for independent action?"

"With one caveat," Jefferson said. "Your mission objective has not changed; Sharon Ingersoll is still your number one priority. Now, that being said, we are currently assuming that she and Sarah are still together, so rescuing Sarah is an acceptable secondary objective. If they are not, you must get Miss Ingersoll out of the country before you take any other action. After that, Allison says you are authorized to go back after Sarah, with your team. You will be completely on your own, though, Noah. If anything goes wrong, we probably won't be able to send anyone out after you."

"I understand that. Thank you."

Noah could hear Jefferson's smile through the phone. "I think that's the first time any of our people have ever said those words to me. Good luck, Camelot." The line went dead.

Noah put the phone into his pocket, just as they heard a

knock on the door. Marco rose and crossed to it quickly to open it.

A woman and three men stood in the hallway, and Noah recognized Jenny Lance despite the fact that her usually black hair was now as blonde as Sarah's. Jenny stood five foot four and, like Sarah, she had the athletic build of a cheerleader. Her bright blue eyes seemed to look right through you, and yet you were certain that she didn't miss a single detail. She stepped into the room and the men followed.

"Noah," she said. "Do you guys know my team? This is Jim Marino, Randy Mitchell and Dave Lange. Guys, this is Noah Wolf, aka Camelot, and you've met Marco before." She turned and looked at Neil. "I don't believe we've had the pleasure?"

"Neil Blessing," Noah said. "My computer man."

Neil nodded once, and the man she had identified as Jim broke into a smile and stepped toward him. "Man, am I glad to meet you," he said, extending a hand. "I've heard of you. The company considers you the best, and they passed on some of your tricks to the rest of us. Your Ghost Money program is absolutely awesome."

Neil smiled, and actually blushed. On one of their very first missions, he had written a program that could cause bank accounting computers to think money had been transferred in, only to vanish at a preset time later. That program had enabled Noah to get close to his target, but it also made it possible for the American government to capture a large supply of black-market nuclear weapons material.

Jenny grinned at the two of them, but then turned to Noah. "I've been briefed," she said. "How can we help?"

"Allison said you already have an idea in mind. Let's

hear it."

She shrugged. "I remember Sarah from the memorial, and it struck me then that we look a little bit alike. Since my hair was already blonde for the last mission, I suggested that maybe I become her older sister and start raising hell at the prison. With any luck, they'll decide they need to shut me up and try to grab me, as well."

Noah nodded his understanding. "Of course, they could just decide to put a bullet in you. That wouldn't exactly be a desirable outcome."

Jenny laughed, and an outsider would have thought it was a laugh of delight. "I'm pretty hard to kill. Besides, I think I can throw enough seductiveness into my act to make someone think I'm more valuable alive. The question is how you're going to be able to track me if that happens."

Noah turned to Neil. "Neil? Any ideas?"

"Well, we don't have any more of the little subdermal trackers we used on Sarah," he said, "and those don't give us any real range, anyway." He turned to his computer and started tapping keys. A moment later, he grinned and turned back to Noah. "There's an interesting little device called the Spark Nano International GPS Tracker. It can bounce signals off any cell tower within range, so we can literally track it in real time, and the battery is good for about three weeks. There's a dealer right here in Bangkok, less than two miles from here. I can have one within an hour."

"How big is it?" Noah asked. "Is it something that's going to be extremely noticeable? If she does get snatched, they're probably going to pat her down and go through her pockets."

Neil grimaced. "Yeah, there's that," he said. He turned

back to the computer and clicked a link. "It's about an inch-and-a-half by three inches, and not quite an inch thick. If they pat her down, they'll find it. Let me see what else..."

"Not where I'll put it, they won't," Jenny said. "And get that look off your face, this is about doing what we have to do. The thing is moisture resistant, right?"

His face red and averted, Neil nodded.

Jenny turned to Lange. "Take Neil and go get one. The sooner we get busy on this, the better I'm gonna like it."

Neil got up and followed Lange out the door to the car, still avoiding letting his eyes meet Jenny's. As the door closed behind them, the woman turned to Noah.

"Cute kid," she said. "How does he cope with what we do?"

"He does okay," Noah said. "He's just not had a lot of experience with women. Try not to traumatize him, would you? I need him able to function."

She laughed again. "Okay, I'll take it easy on the kid. Now, here's what I got in mind. As soon as he gets me set up, I'm going down to that prison to start raising all kinds of hell. I'm going to demand to see my sister, and when they tell me she's escaped I'm going to go completely nuts on them. If the prison officials allowed the pimps to come in and pick who they wanted, they're probably not going to want to get police involved with me. I'm betting they'll call those same guys to try to make me disappear, too."

Noah nodded. "There's at least a good chance of that," he said. "Of course, that doesn't mean you'll be taken to the same place they were."

"Who cares? We're not going to wait till they take me to their slaughterhouse, we're going to take them down and make them spill their guts. Geneva Convention and humane conduct rules be damned, we're going to make those bastards talk. Right?"

"Right. It's as good a plan as I can come up with." He looked at Mitchell and Marino. "You guys, Marco and I will be keeping her under surveillance the best we can, while Neil rides with Lange and watches the computer. If we lose her, he'll be able to guide us back on track, but we're going to do our best to keep her in sight. Then we'll take them down at the first possible chance." He thought for a moment. "We need a place to take them, somewhere we can do our questioning without anyone overhearing."

Marino picked up his computer bag and set it on the table beside Neil's laptop, opened it up and turned it on. "Give me a few minutes," he said, "and I'll find us a place."

Five minutes later he pointed to an image on his screen. "This place is about forty minutes out to the southeast, in a rural area. It's an abandoned clothing factory, and there's nobody around it for miles, unless it's got squatters. I ran it through law enforcement databases, and there are no police reports connected to it, so I think it's isolated enough for our purposes."

"It'll do," Noah said. "Any squatters will probably leave in a hurry when we show up, and they're not likely to want any contact with police." He looked at Lange. "I know you've got a car, but we're going to need more vehicles. Let me make a call."

He took out his phone and called Knapp. The operative answered on the first ring, even though he probably hadn't gotten any sleep at all.

"Darrell, this is Camelot. I need some wheels and some weapons."

"I'm your guy. What kind of transportation?"

"I'm thinking motorcycles, four of them. We're likely to

need maneuverability, and two wheelers get around this city better than four-wheelers."

"No problem, I can have them to you in a couple of hours. What kind of weapons?"

"Four Glock forties, maybe a couple of baby Uzis. Two magazines for each, and silencers for the Glocks. If we need more than that, it will mean we're in serious trouble. I also want some communications gear. Do you have access to something like earpiece setups? Small and easily concealed, but with a decent range?"

"I think I've got just the thing. Four sets?"

"Unless you can make it six."

"Okay, give me two hours. We'll deliver it all to your hotel, right?"

"That'll be perfect." He ended the call and put the phone back into his pocket. "I'm guessing you guys can ride, right?"

All three of the men nodded. "Man," Marco said, "I was born on two wheels. I can ride anything."

Neil and Dave Lange returned after almost an hour, and Neil set to work immediately programming the tracker. Its battery was fully charged, so it was only twenty minutes later when Neil blushingly handed it to Jenny. She took it without a word and stepped into the bathroom.

When she stepped out a moment later, she looked Neil directly in the eye. "I take it you're getting a clear signal?"

Neil swallowed, but nodded. He was saved from having to speak by a knock on the door.

Darrell Knapp stood there, and at his invitation they all followed him down the stairs and out the front door. A cargo van was parked a couple of blocks away, and he led the way to it.

"I rounded up the quickest bikes I could find," he said as he threw up the rear door, "so you've got four Honda 400s." The men quickly set about unloading the quartet of sport bikes, while Darrell picked up a pair of briefcases and handed them to Noah. "The rest of your order is in these," he said. "Anything else I can do for you?"

"Not unless you got any leads on what happened to my operative."

Darrell grimaced and looked abashed. "Unfortunately, I don't. I'm still trying, but this is a real gray area here in Thailand. The worst part is that it isn't even entirely illegal; unless the women speak up about being forced, there isn't a whole lot that can be done about it."

Noah nodded. "Then this will do. Keep me posted if you find anything out."

Darrell tucked his chin and climbed into the passenger seat of the van. It drove away a moment later, and they pushed the motorcycles into the parking area of the hotel, then checked their fuel tanks. All of them were full and ready to go.

"Well," Jenny said when they got back up to the hotel room, "we've got everything we need. Why don't we get started now?"

Noah looked at her. "It's Sunday," he said. "What you need to do is go to the visitor registration office at the prison and ask to see your sister. They'll probably give you the runaround for a while, but sooner or later they'll have to tell you she's gone. The official story is that she escaped last night, so be ready to go into your act."

"Don't worry about me," she said, "acting is how I get close to my targets. Did you know I went to Julliard? I was all set for a career in movies and theater before my real little sister was killed. She was raped and murdered by a sixteen-year-old boy in New York City. It was part of his gang initiation."

"And you took action?" Noah asked.

Jenny nodded gravely. "Animals like that need to be removed from the gene pool. I killed him and all three of his brothers, who were just as bad as he was. Would have killed his parents, too, so they couldn't produce any more, but I'd struck early in the morning when there should have been no one else around. Unfortunately, one of the neighbors had stayed home sick that morning. She heard the screaming and called the police. There was a squad car just a block away, and they cornered me. I was convicted on all counts, sentenced to die and that's when Allison came to visit me. I'm pretty sure you know how the rest turns out."

Noah cocked his head to one side and looked at her for a moment. "Sounds like you let your anger get the best of you. I'm kind of surprised she recruited you, under the circumstances."

Jenny laughed. "Oh, no, you got it all wrong. I didn't do this in a fit of anger; I waited and planned it out for almost six months, and the closer it got to the time I chose to do it, the more excited I got. The cops that arrested me put in their report that I was obviously enjoying myself, and that's what got Allison's attention." She shrugged. "Turns out I was a closet sadist. I happen to enjoy killing, so this is the best possible work for me to be in. I get to indulge my passion and get paid for it at the same time."

Noah nodded. "That makes sense, then. Just don't kill your captors until we get a chance to get information out of them."

The pretty woman smiled again. "Oh, no worries. Torturing information out of someone's sort of like foreplay, for me. I like to string it out and make it last."

Noah looked at the others. "Lange, you'll take your car and Neil will go with you. Neil, take your computer so you can keep track of Jenny for me." He opened the briefcases and handed Neil and the driver each one of the mini-Uzis, then passed out the rest of the weapons and the earpieces. Each of the men clipped one to his ear and turned it on.

"Everybody on?" Noah asked, and all of them nodded. "Okay, we're ready. Jenny, you should take a taxi to the prison, it's quicker than the ferry. We'll all rendezvous at a little restaurant close by, so we'll be ready to move the moment something happens."

Jenny giggled, and Neil shivered. "Cool, baby," she said. "Let's do this."

SIXTEEN

Noah and the other men were gathered around the table near the front door of the restaurant. Jenny had entered visitor registration more than an hour earlier, and they'd seen no sign of her since then. Neil had brought his computer and was checking the screen periodically to see if she had moved, but the blip that indicated her presence only wandered back and forth around the registration office area.

"She's moving around a little more the last few minutes," he said. "I guess she's doing the getting mad bit."

"She does it well," Mitchell said. "Really well. She can put on a mood faster than she can put on a hat."

Mitchell's phone suddenly rang, and he answered it on the second ring. He then held the phone away from his ear, because Jenny's voice could be heard screaming frantically.

"Daddy! Daddy, I'm here in Bangkok, at the prison where they took Kayla, but they're telling me she's gone! Daddy, they're trying to tell me she broke out, and you know Kayla couldn't do anything like that. Daddy, what do I do?"

Mitchell looked surprised, so Noah reached over and

took the phone. "Lisa, calm down," he said. "What do you mean? Somebody said she escaped?"

If Jenny was surprised that Noah had taken on the act as her father, it didn't show in her voice. "Yes! Daddy, you know that can't be true, Kayla is just too soft for anything like that. What do I do?"

"Honey, you go back in there and tell those people they're lying, and you don't leave them until you know where your sister is! I don't care what you have to do, you find out what's going on, okay?"

Jenny sniffled. "Okay," she said, "okay, Daddy. I'll do my best."

He ended the call, and Noah handed the phone back to Mitchell. "Sorry about that," he said, "but you can't leave her hanging. If she calls you with an act like that, you have to respond instantly."

Mitchell rolled his eyes. "Yeah, well, usually she gives me some kind of warning before she pulls that sort of thing. I just wasn't expecting it, this time."

"I understand," Noah said, "but that's why it was easier for me to just take over and do it. If I tried to coach you, someone on her end might have overheard."

"So what do you think that means?" Neil asked.

"It means she's gotten to the point they've admitted Sarah isn't there. This is where she's got to make herself as annoying as possible."

Marino chuckled. "Oh, trust me, she's good at that."

They sat there sipping coffee and tea for another two hours, until Mitchell's phone rang once again. He answered it again, but then he frowned. "It's Jenny," he said. "They ran her out and told her to come back tomorrow morning."

Noah nodded. "Then that's what she'll do," he said. "Tell her to take a taxi back to the hotel, and we'll meet her there. Neil, keep watching, just in case something happens before we get back with her."

"I'm on it," Neil said.

The men sat there a few more minutes, then got up and paid their tabs. They wandered out to the street, and a moment later they were all moving back toward the hotel. Lange drove a different route than the one taken by the men on the bikes, but they all arrived back at the hotel around the same time.

Jenny had arranged a room for herself and her team, and managed to put it on the same floor as Noah's. She was standing in the doorway when they came up the stairs, and they all followed her inside.

"I think I got their attention," she said. "The clerk on duty made several phone calls, then told me I had to come back tomorrow. He said he'll make sure his supervisor is there to talk to me in the morning. What do you bet the supervisor is connected to the *Nay Thas*?"

"You could be right," Noah said. "Just to be on the safe side, we'll send the car and two of the bikes ahead in the morning, and then Randy and I will follow your taxi. It's always possible they followed you back here, could try to snatch you in the morning."

"Great thought," Neil said. "What if they try to grab her during the night?"

"Then they'll get a big surprise," Jenny said. "Between me and the guys, they'd need to bring a platoon."

Neil shook his head and turned to go back to their own room. "Let me know when it's time for dinner," he said. "Don't know about anyone else, but I'm hungry."

"We just left a freakin' restaurant," Marco said, grinning at him. "Why didn't you order something to eat while we were there?"

"Because then if something happened," Neil said, "I'd have to walk away from food. Do you know how hard that would be?" He stomped into the room and shut the door behind him.

Marco rolled his eyes. "I swear, that kid is the Galloping Gizzard! I think he could eat a car."

Noah looked at him a moment, and turned back to Jenny. "Neil's right, we should be thinking about getting something to eat. We got caught up in the heat of everything and skipped breakfast, and none of us have even had lunch."

"They got room service in this joint?" Jenny asked.

"No, but there's a restaurant downstairs, and several more nearby."

"Then let's just send a couple of the boys out to grab some food and bring it back. I don't really feel like going out right now."

Marco and Dave volunteered to go fetch food, so Noah went back to his room and lay down on the bed. Neil was sitting at his computer like always, and Noah noticed that he had what looked like a satellite image on the screen.

"What's that?" He asked.

"I hacked into a satellite," Neil said. "NSA keeps one over Bangkok. Codename Lemonwood. I'm going through its images for last night, see if I can find out where that van might've gone."

"Excellent thinking," Noah said. "Let me know if you find anything."

"I haven't yet, but I'm pretty sure I will. I just had to

figure out its encoding, the way it records its timestamps. It takes a still photo every two seconds, and its lens can cover a pretty big area. All I've got to do is find the moment when Sarah was loaded into that van and then scan through the images and keep myself zeroed in on it." He tapped the keys for a couple more seconds, then grinned. "Okay, there's the van. Good grief, the resolution on this camera is so good I can even see us hiding behind the bushes."

Noah sat up on his bed. "What about Sarah?"

"I'm ticking forward one image at a time. The van pulled up at 11:38 and twenty-two seconds. Two frames later I see two men getting out. They're walking toward the front door, looks like somebody opened it for them when they got there. Now they must be inside, I can't see them anymore. Another man just got out of the van and is standing beside it. Going through the frames—nothing, nothing, nothing—okay, I've gone four minutes ahead, still nothing, one man still standing beside the van. Skipping ahead, one minute—no change, two minutes—no change. Ahead one more minute, still no change—another minute, no change."

Noah heard the clicking of the keys and then Neil suddenly sat up straight. "Okay, there! Two men coming out, looks like four women, the guy at the van opens the back door and the women get in. Door is closed, the two men go back inside. Skipping a minute, two minutes, three minutes—no change so far."

Noah stood and walked over to stand beside him, looking over his shoulder at the computer screen. "This is brilliant, Neil," he said.

"It'll be brilliant if it helps us find Sarah. I'm at five minutes, no change—six minutes, the door is open, the front door of the prison is open. Okay, I'm backing up a couple frames. There's the door opening, nobody in sight yet—going frame by frame, now. Bingo, here we go. That's two men and two women, coming out the front door. Next frame, the door is closed and they're moving toward the van. Back doors are opened, and the two women are put inside. Doors close, all three men climb in the front of the van. That would be the point where we saw Sarah's tracker start to move, because there goes the van. It's moving up the road, and look, there we are looking like idiots as it goes by."

"Stay on it," Noah said. "How far can you follow it with this?"

"I'm zoomed way in," Neil said. "If I zoom all the way out, I can see pretty much all of Asia, but I can't track the van from that far out. I'm gonna stay on it, but this is going to take a while."

Noah nodded his head. "Just keep at it as long as you can. Even having a direction to look in would help." He turned and walked to the door, then stepped out and knocked on Jenny's door. Neil could hear him giving her the short version, and then he was back with Jenny, Jim and Randy in tow.

Jim Marino pulled a chair away from the table and sat down beside Neil. "Someday," he said, "you gotta show me how to do this. I always thought I was good, but I can't get into the satellites."

"Be quiet, I'm focusing on the van. Look, it's moving along this little side street, no, it turned onto the main road, 3110. Headed south in the fast lane. I'm going to jump ahead one minute—no, lost it, going back. There it is, I'm sticking to frame by frame."

"You're doing great, Neil," Noah said. "Stay on it."

"I am, I am," Neil shot back. "Look, it just turned onto the main superhighway. Still moving south, still in the fast lane. I'm gonna try jumping a few seconds at a time, if I back off the zoom a bit I should still be able to keep the van in each frame. Yeah, there it is, still south, still south, looks like they might have sped up a bit."

Marco and Dave came in with a couple of buckets full of fried chicken and curried rice, and started passing the food around. Neil bit into a chicken leg while he kept up his running commentary, and everyone else gathered as close as they could to watch the computer screen.

For almost 20 minutes, Neil managed to track the van as it made its way south and out of the city, finally turning onto Highway 3, one of the major highways in the country. He was able to watch until the van moved into a rural area about forty miles to the south. Once it moved under the cover of trees, however, it seemed to be lost.

Neil was cursing and pounding on the desk, but his computer and the satellite didn't respond to his threats. After casting about for another half hour, he finally looked at Noah.

"I lost her, boss," he said. And then he burst into tears.

Noah laid a hand on his shoulder. "No, you didn't," he said. "You've given us our best lead yet. We know that her captors were taking her towards Pattaya, and that's one of their major operational markets. Sooner or later, we're going to find someone who can tell us exactly where she's been taken, but this puts us ahead of the game. We already have an idea of the general direction, now what we need are specifics."

Jenny patted Neil on the back. "You done good, there, Neil. Now, with any luck, this so-called supervisor I'm meeting in the morning will send the same animals after me, and then we'll be able to get down and dirty with them."

"But this doesn't help," Neil said through his tears. "She can be anywhere between where I lost the van and the South China Sea."

"It does help," Noah said. "Whatever answers Jenny gets tomorrow, we'll know if they're being honest or not because we already know part of the truth. We know she went south, so if they claim she went north or east, we know it's time to put on the pressure."

Marco handed Neil a couple of napkins and the kid wiped his eyes. He suddenly seemed to realize that he had broken down in front of them all, and his face blushed bright red. "Look," he said, "I'm just tired, all right? I don't normally start crying like that, you got it?"

Jenny smiled at him. "Of course not," she said. "We can tell."

SEVENTEEN

S
arah had been surprised when the boat landed on one of the most beautiful white sand beaches she had ever seen. The vessel was propelled right onto the beach, and the men began yelling at the girls to get out as soon as it stopped. She, Sharon and the others hopped over the side into the knee-deep water, and waded onto the shore.

"This place almost looks like a resort," Sharon whispered, "but somehow I don't think it is."

"No, I'm sure you're right," Sarah replied. "Just stay calm and let's try to survive this."

One of the men started walking into the forest that seemed to cover most of the island, and the Asian girls fell into line behind him. The other two men pushed Sarah and Sharon, and they caught on. They got into line and followed the other girls.

The forest was dense, but the path seemed pretty well worn. They walked about a mile, Sarah guessed, and finally came to a group of simple earthen huts. There was an open area near them with some picnic tables, and several women were sitting around them, watching the new-comers arrive. Some of them were laughing and smiling, but Sarah noticed that the smiles didn't seem to reach their eyes.

The man leading their group stopped and pointed at one of the tables, and Sarah and Sharon followed as the other girls sat down. A moment later, an older woman came out of one of the huts and set bowls of rice, chicken and fish in front of each of them. The food was fresh and actually smelled pretty good, so when the other girls began shoving it into their mouths, Sarah did likewise.

"Eat up," she said to Sharon. "It's all about keeping up your strength, not getting hurt. If we're going to survive this, if we're going to be alive when Noah comes to get us, we got to do whatever it takes." She took another bite and then grinned. "Tell you what, this isn't half bad."

Sharon gave her a sour look, but picked up her own bowl and began to eat. "They could at least give us silverware," she said. The comment struck Sarah as funny, and she began to giggle; a moment later they were both trying to suppress their laughter.

One of the men noticed and came to stand over them. "You laugh? Something funny?" he asked in broken English. The simple absurdity of the situation was too much, and Sarah began laughing even harder. The man stood there and stared at her for several seconds, then turned around and stomped away.

As soon as they had finished eating, the six of them were pulled away from the table and pushed into one of the huts. There were pallets inside, just as they had seen in the sleeping rooms at the prison, and Sarah quickly claimed two of them for herself and Sharon. "Looks like maybe we get to rest a bit more," she said. "I don't know about you, but I could stand a few more hours of sleep."

"Yeah," Sharon said. "It's bound to be more comfortable than the bottom of that van."

The two of them lay down on the pallets and closed their eyes, but the other girls began talking. Sarah ignored them for a few moments, then opened one eye and found Sharon looking at her. "I wish we could understand what they're saying," Sarah said. "We might get some idea of what's in store for us."

"My own imagination is doing enough of that," Sharon said. "I don't think I want to know any more than I already do."

"Well, in that case let's just try to ignore them." She closed her eyes again and tried to relax herself into sleep.

She never made it. They were only in the hut for about fifteen minutes when one of the men pulled aside the curtain it used for a door and shouted at them all to come out. Sarah didn't understand his words, but the way the other girls responded made it clear what he wanted. She and Sharon followed and lined up with the others when they got outside.

There were several men wandering around, and most of them were carrying automatic rifles. One of them looked at the two American girls and seemed to smile. "Westerners," he said clearly in English. "You'll bring us some good money." He paused, and Sarah felt his eyes roaming her body.

"I am Pak," he said. He walked closer, until he was standing in front of Sarah. "You are lucky," he said, "that we took you out of that hell hole of a prison. You would not have lasted long there, not as pretty as you are. The Toms there would fight over you, and sooner or later one of them would become jealous. It would be a shame if you were killed over such foolishness."

Sarah felt a shiver go down her spine, as it dawned on her that such a fate might have awaited Sharon if nothing had been done to rescue her, but she didn't see their current situation as anything lucky. "And what you want us for is better?"

"Of course," he said, his smile widening. "You will be adored by many men, and lavished with gifts. You will earn money greater than you could hope for in your own country, and you will probably move in the circles of power. Princes and Presidents will come to you, and perhaps one will choose to make you his own. Is that not a better fate than the one we saved you from?"

Sarah looked into his eyes for a moment and realized that this man actually believed what he was saying. She decided to play up to his conceit and look for any advantage it might give her.

"Okay, maybe," she said, chewing her bottom lip. "But why would you want to let others have us? Maybe you might want us for yourself."

Sharon's eyes went wide as she looked at Sarah, but she didn't say anything. The man chuckled.

"Little flower, I am not a man who craves women," he said. "I seek wealth and power, and being a purveyor of such fine goods is what brings me both. Don't worry yourself, though, I won't let you go to a dog." He turned his eyes to Sharon, who forced herself to smile. "You will both serve well at the feet of the powerful, I am sure, and if you are as smart as you are lovely, you will live long, happy lives."

He turned away and barked an order in Thai to one of the other men, who looked at the two girls and grinned. Both of them cringed inwardly, as the new man came toward them.

"This is Cho," the first man said. "He speaks your language almost as well as I, so he will begin teaching you what is expected of you. Do not give him trouble, and he will not hurt you."

Sarah looked at Cho, a short, stocky man with a scarred face, then turned back to Pak. "And can you tell me what it is that he plans to teach us?"

Pak smiled, and the evil in it sent a shiver down the spines of both girls. "He will teach you that you are nothing," he said, and then he walked away.

Cho came to stand in front of them and his own eyes drank in their figures and faces. "You come with me now," he said, and then he turned and walked off toward a stand of trees.

Sarah looked at Sharon and grimaced. "We have to survive," she said. "And we can survive, no matter what. Everything depends on us being alive and unhurt when Noah gets here."

Sharon stared at her for a second, then nodded slowly as she started to follow Cho. "Survive," she said. "Just survive."

The two of them caught up with him a moment later, as he led them into a clearing that was separated from the rest of the compound by a wall of trees. There was nothing in the clearing but a series of boxes, roughly four feet in every dimension. The tops were hinged and had been thrown open, and Cho simply pointed at the first one as he looked at Sarah. "You go in," he said.

Sarah looked at the box, then turned to stare at Cho. "In the box? Why?"

Cho didn't bother to answer. He simply grabbed her by her neck and one leg, picked her up and dropped her unceremoniously into the box. A moment later the top slammed shut, and she heard the clicking that meant a pin went into the hasp that would hold it shut.

"You go in," she heard Cho say, and then she heard what sounded like a sob from Sharon, followed by a squeal as she was apparently subjected to the same treatment. The other box slammed shut, and another pin was put into place.

Sarah pressed her face to a small gap between the boards that made up the box and saw Cho walking away. She listened for any other sounds, but all she could hear was Sharon crying in the box beside her.

"Sharon?" Sarah called softly. "Sharon, try to hold it together. I know what this is, they're trying to break our spirits. This is kind of a good thing, because it means they won't be doing anything else to us for a while." She stopped and listened, but Sharon didn't respond. "Sharon, hang on. Trust me, Noah is working on getting us out of here already. We might be a little uncomfortable for a while, but at least we're not being raped at the moment."

There was silence for a moment, that she heard Sharon clear her throat. "I guess now is a bad time to mention that I'm a little claustrophobic," she said, and Sarah heard a soft chuckle. "How long do you think they'll leave us in here? I'm gonna need a bathroom sometime soon."

Sarah grimaced, then looked around the inside of her own box the best she could. A little light came through the gaps, but as far as she could tell there were no holes in the bottom of the box. In fact, there were some awfully nasty-looking stains down there, and the box smelled pretty rank.

"I doubt they're going to offer us a potty break," she said. "Psychologically, it helps to break a person's spirit if they're forced to live in their own excrement. They'll probably offer to let us out at some point, but only if we agree to whatever demands they want to put on us, but that won't happen soon. With any luck, Noah and the guys will track us down before we get to that point."

"You really seem to have a lot of faith in this Noah," Sharon said. "Did you see all the men with guns out there?"

"Yeah, I saw them. Most of them are carrying AK-74s, or some sort of copy of them, and the way they handle them makes me think they had military training. Noah will do a careful recon of the situation before he comes in, but I doubt these guys will give him much of a problem. It may sound hard to believe, but I've seen him walk into much deadlier situations and come out of them alive."

"Yeah? And what about everybody else in that situation? Did they come out alive, too?"

Sarah thought back to a couple of the incidents she was referring to. "Sharon, twice I've seen him walk into traps that were supposed to kill him, just to get me out. Noah is probably one of the most dangerous men alive, especially to anyone he considers an enemy. By taking us, these people have interfered with his mission. That makes them the enemy of the moment, and I doubt any of them will survive what's coming."

EIGHTEEN

D ave and Neil drove away in the rented Toyota at just after eight the following morning, with Marco and Marino following on the Hondas. Noah and Randy Mitchell got on their own bikes and watched as Jenny climbed into one of the waiting taxis. When the car started moving, they pulled out to follow but kept a few other cars between them.

There were no incidents on the way to the prison, so the men made rendezvous at the same restaurant they had used the day before. They sat where they could watch as Jenny got out of the taxi and headed into the visitors registration office. A moment later, Mitchell's phone rang and he held it out to Noah.

Noah answered the phone. "Hello? Lisa?"

"Yes, Daddy, it's me," Jenny said. "I'm back at the prison and waiting to meet this supervisor. Hopefully he can tell me something about what happened to Kayla. I just wanted to let you know what was going on, and I'll call you as soon as I know anything more."

"Okay, honey," Noah said. "I'll be right here by the phone."

The call ended and Noah handed the phone back to Mitchell. "Waiting for the supervisor," he said. "We might as well have some breakfast."

Like the day before, Neil had his computer open on the table. Anyone walking casually past would have thought he was playing some sort of video game, but the display on the screen actually showed him an accurate map of the city of Bangkok, with a blinking purple dot that told him precisely where Jenny was at any given moment. Neil had simply added some graphics and lettering so that it wouldn't be a recognizable map even to a native.

They ordered breakfast, keeping it simple and easy, and chitchatted about mundane things as they ate. Marco and Mitchell were talking about the latest MLB game, while Neil and Marino were going on and on about various on-line games they liked to play in their free time. Noah and Lange were discussing trends in automobile design.

An hour passed with no word from Jenny, but Neil assured them she was still in the visitors registration office. The little blip moved around enough to indicate that she was either impatient or angry, and Noah decided that they had better prepare for something to happen soon. He paid their tabs and sent everyone back to their vehicles. "It's just a hunch," he said, "but I'd rather be ready if something happens. Unless she leaves alone, we have to assume that someone is making a play to grab her. As soon as we can stop them and take them down, we do so."

The four motorcycles were parked close together, so the men sat on them and talked while they waited for the next development. Neil and Dave were in the car, about fifty yards away, and Noah had positioned himself so that he could see Neil clearly. If anything happened on the computer screen, Neil would tell them immediately through the radio headsets they were all wearing.

Suddenly, Neil cocked his head to one side, and Noah

waved a finger to tell the others to be quiet. A second later, Neil's voice came through the headsets. "She just went into a back room, and if I'm reading it right, it might be the storeroom we were going to use to go in. The only way she could go there is if they took her, that's not a place she could've wandered into on her own."

"Agreed," Noah said. "Keep watching. They may be trying to rough her up a bit."

"They'll regret it," Mitchell said. "She may be little, but she can kick ass like a professional wrestler."

"In her own persona, yes," Noah said, "but in this case she's just a worried big sister of a missing girl. I doubt she's going to show off her combat skills, not unless it's absolutely necessary."

"I'm not seeing any sign of frantic activity," Neil said, "but that thing's only able to give me a position within three feet. If she's sitting down and getting smacked around, it might not register."

"Just watch," Noah said. "Let us know if anything changes."

A few more minutes passed as they waited, and then Neil called out again. "Okay, she's moving," he said. "Coming toward the front door, she should be stepping out about—now."

The door of the prison visitors office opened and Jenny stepped out, but she was not alone. Two men in uniforms were walking alongside her, and one of them was holding onto her arm. Noah turned on the video camera function of his cell phone and aimed it at her, zooming in as far as he could. She was smiling and talking to the man who was holding her arm, and her other hand held her purse. She appeared to be completely unconcerned about being taken somewhere.

The three of them turned into a parking area and the second man opened the back door of a car. Jenny slid inside and the man who had been holding her arm got in beside her. The other man closed the door, then got behind the wheel and started the car.

"This is it," Noah said. "Neil, I want you guys to hang back. You just make sure you let us know if they make any sudden changes in direction. Let's do this. We need to take them as soon as they reach any kind of secluded area."

"Roger that," Marco said, and he was echoed by all of the others.

The four motorcycles followed the car that was holding Jenny, weaving from lane to lane so that it was never obvious. There were so many motorcycles on the road that it would've been nearly impossible to identify a tail that involved more than one. Neil and Dave, in the rental car, were a couple of blocks further back. They didn't need to keep the car in sight.

The car turned onto the main road, 3110, and went south, just as the van that had taken Sarah had done. Once again, there were enough motorcycles on the road that the presence of four more of them was not suspicious, so the driver paid no attention as Noah and the men with him kept the car in view.

Half an hour later, the car turned onto Highway 3 and accelerated, moving into the fast lane and proceeding south. Neil's voice came through the headsets. "Boss, I think they're taking her to the same place," he said. "They're going the same way the van did, anyway."

"I know," Noah said, "but don't make assumptions. Whoever those men are, they know something about what happened to Sarah. I want to stop them and question them, without letting them notify anybody else that something is happening."

"Okay, then," Neil said. "We're coming up on an exit, and it's the road that leads to that old clothing factory we were planning to use for questioning. Can you think of any way to make them get off?"

"I think so," Noah said. He twisted the throttle on the motorcycle and roared up beside the driver's window, then reached into his jacket and produced the Glock. The driver had glanced over at him when he suddenly appeared, and now his eyes went wide at the sight of the pistol. Noah used it to indicate that he should take the next exit, but the man shook his head stubbornly.

Jenny, in the backseat, suddenly used her elbow on the jaw of the man beside her, then reached up and put a hand on the driver's throat. Noah couldn't hear what she said, but the driver's eyes went wide and he began nodding furiously. His turn signal came on, and Noah fell back to follow the car off the exit ramp with the others.

Five minutes later, they pulled into the parking lot of the old factory and circled around behind it. There was a section of wall missing, and they were able to drive the vehicles right inside. When they stopped, the driver found himself surrounded by armed men riding motorcycles, so he didn't offer any resistance. Another car pulled into the building and parked, and two men got out, both of them holding Uzis, which only strengthened his determination not to antagonize his captors. Noah and Randy Mitchell kept their guns trained on the driver as Marco pulled him out of the car, and then Jenny opened the back door and stepped out.

"Took you guys long enough," she said. "I thought you were going to wait till we got to wherever they were taking me."

"I thought about it," Noah said, "but that might have been a mistake. We have no idea how many men they may have there, or how much security. We can't afford to walk into a trap, we still have a mission to complete."

Marco and Mitchell grabbed the man in the back seat and dragged him out of the car; he seemed to be regaining consciousness as they propped him on its hood. He looked around at the faces of the men, then his gaze focused on Jenny again.

"What is this?" he asked. "Were we not taking you to your sister? Why do your friends attack us?"

"Well, you see," Jenny said, "it's like this. She's not really my sister, and I'm not really a sweet young thing from Omaha. I do, however, want to get her back, and I'm prepared to do absolutely anything necessary to make you tell me where she is." She looked from one of the men to the other. "So, who wants to answer my questions without getting hurt?"

The two men looked at each other, glanced at the other men standing around them and then looked at Jenny. "You do not know what you are doing," the man from the backseat said. "We will not help you."

Jenny smiled brightly. "Oh, I was hoping you would say that," she said. She reached into her purse and took out a small folding knife, then set her purse on the ground and opened it. The blade was only a couple of inches long, but it was obviously razor-sharp. "Now, something you should know about me is that I absolutely love torturing people. The longer you hold out without telling me what I want to know, the happier I'm going to be. The thing is, though, sooner or later you are going to tell me. Now, you can make me happy and drag this on until you're barely even alive, or you can save yourself a lot of pain and suffering by answering my questions right away. It's entirely up to you, it doesn't matter to me either way."

The man who had done all the talking shook his head. "As I tell you, we will not help you."

Jenny jumped up and down and clapped her hands. "Oh, goody," she said. "Oh, this is going to be so much fun!" She wiggled a couple of fingers, and Randy Mitchell and Dave Lange stepped forward. "Eenie, meenie, minie, mo...Which one of you should I start with?" She pointed to the man who had not yet spoken. "You? Yeah, let's start with you!" Lange and Mitchell each took hold of one of his arms, while Marco and Jim Marino held onto the other man.

Lange had hold of the man by the back of his neck and his left arm, while Mitchell held onto his right. They lifted him off the hood of the car to make him stand. The man looked at Jenny nervously, but did not speak. Jenny was looking him over from head to toe, and the expression on her face was one of utter, childish delight.

"Where to start, where to start," she muttered. "Maybe your ears? Ears are pretty sensitive, they might do. Or I could go for your eyes, nobody likes to lose an eye, right? Hmmm, so many choices." Her right hand, holding the knife, suddenly flashed forward so quickly that it was nearly invisible. The tip of the blade caught in the cup of the man's left ear and sliced through. Blood splattered, but it was a couple of seconds before the man actually realized what happened.

NINETEEN

He managed to reach up and put a hand to his ear, and it came away bloodied. He looked at the blood on his hand, then at Jenny, and the expression on his face became one of horror. "You crazy lady," he said.

"Oh, yes, I am," Jenny said brightly. "This is how I get my jollies. Now, that was just one cut and I figure you're good for about thirty-five more of them before you lose enough blood to pass out. Of course, there are a few places I could cut that would make you bleed out faster, but I'm gonna make this last a while. So here's how the game is played, okay? I'm going to ask you a question, and if you answer me truthfully, I stop cutting. If you don't, then I'm going to cut you again, and we are going to keep this up until you answer my question. Ready? Here comes the question. Where did they take Kayla Maguire?"

The man with the bleeding ear looked at his compatriot for a second, but then looked at the ground. Neither of them spoke, and Jenny suddenly reached out and grabbed the man's right hand. It happened so quickly that even Noah was caught by surprise, as she raked the blade down his index finger, shaving off the flesh and the nail and leaving the bone exposed.

This time, the man reacted instantly, screaming loudly, but the screams only echoed off the concrete walls. Jenny let him shriek for a moment, while he tried to hold his finger and make the pain and bleeding stop.

She glanced at the other man. "Are you ready to play yet?" He simply looked at the floor, refusing to even acknowledge her question. She turned back to the man who was crying so loudly.

"Where did they take Kayla Maguire?" Jenny asked again, and the man stared into her face. He opened his mouth once, but then closed it again. Jenny cocked her head to one side and looked at him with a curious expression. "Honey, are you sure you want to go through more of this? Believe me, I enjoy it, so I don't mind—I just thought you might want to think it over."

The man pulled himself together the best he could, still holding his injured finger while his ear continued to bleed profusely. He pointed his eyes straight ahead, and his expression told her that he was refusing to answer.

Jenny stepped up close to him; the man was short enough that she was almost nose-to-nose with him. "At this point," she said softly, "there is a chance you can survive. If I carry this much further, though, that chance will get smaller and smaller and smaller. Are you really willing to die for the people who steal young girls and turn them into slaves? Are you really willing to die for the *Nay Thas*?"

Though he swallowed hard, the man's expression did not change. He continued to stare straight ahead, and Jenny stepped back a few inches just before her hand flashed again, and the blade of the knife sliced across his left eye.

This time, it was all they could do to hold onto him, and

the shrieks of pain and rage that came from him seemed loud enough to break the walls of the building, but they stood. His free hand, the one with the fingernail cut off, came up to cover his ruined eyeball, and Jenny stepped up to him again. She looked into his one remaining eye, which was wide and staring at her. "Can you see it in my face? Can you tell how much I enjoy this? Can you tell I'm getting off on it every time I hurt you? All you got to do to stop this is tell me what I want to know. Where did they take Kayla Maguire?"

His good eye was blinking rapidly, but he did his best to glare at her with it. Jenny stared into it for a moment, then turned to look at the other man. "Are you going to let him continue to suffer? If we turn you guys loose right now, there's a chance he's going to survive. You tell me what I want to know, and I'll let you go. You can take him to a hospital, because he's going to need antibiotics in a hurry. His finger bone is exposed to the air, infections are already setting in. Are you willing to help him?"

The man looked at his friend, who was still doing his best to stare straight ahead. "If we tell you what you want to know," he said, "those you seek will punish us. We are already dead men. What you have done to him will ensure that we will die."

"Is that so?" Jenny asked. "And do you believe that's fair? Is that right? No one can endure the kind of pain I'm inflicting on him for long without giving me what I want, you know that. Is it right that the two of you should be punished because I forced him to talk?"

"I do not speak of right or wrong. I speak only of what will be."

Jenny nodded. "Then why not get your revenge on them? If you tell me what I want to know, the people you're afraid of are going to die. They won't be able to come after you, or your friend. Where did they take Kayla Maguire?"

The man who had spoken looked at her, and then he sighed. "If you kill them, there will only be more. Perhaps they will still punish us, but perhaps not. You know of the *Nay Thas*, so you must know what they are capable of. If you plan to kill them, then you will need more men than these." He squinted at her. "You are American? American agents?"

"Nope," Jenny said. "We're just some people who've already lost girls we love to those monsters. Your government can't stop them, nobody else seems to be able to stop them, so we decided to take the matter into our own hands. Now, I'm going to give you one more chance. You tell me where they took her, and then you and your friend can leave here. Are you stupid enough to pass that up?"

He sighed once more. "The *Nay Thas* is very powerful. Much of our government is involved, even the Royal Navy. These women were taken to *Khram Yai*, but you will never be able to bring them back."

Jenny glanced over at Neil, who was pecking away at his computer on the hood of the car. "Whiz Kid? Any idea where that is?"

"Oh, hell, yeah," Neil said. "*Khram Yai* island, in Pattaya Bay. It's owned and under the jurisdiction of the Royal Navy, but it's only used for occasional ground combat training exercises. It's maybe two hours from here."

Jenny looked back at the man who had answered her and smiled. "Well, it sounds like you told me the truth," she said. "For that, you get your reward." She turned to Randy Mitchell and held out a hand, and he passed her his Glock automatic.

Jenny jacked the slide to make sure there was one in the chamber, then pointed the gun at the man's forehead and pulled the trigger. The one eye of his friend went wide, but then Jenny's second bullet passed through his own brain.

"Geez," Neil yelled, his own eyes as wide as they could be. "I thought you said you were going to let them go?"

"That's the carrot," Jenny said. "You have to give them something to hope for, then you use the stick—that's me —to push them toward it. Between the pain and suffering I give them and the hope that they'll live through it and survive, sooner or later they give in and give me what I want."

"But you killed them!"

Jenny threw a quizzical look at him. "Of course I did," she said, "they would've tipped off the *Nay Thas* that we were coming. We can't have that."

Neil stared at her for a couple of seconds, then turned and leaned over the fender of the car and began retching. Marco went to him and put a hand on his shoulder, but Neil pushed him away.

The bodies of the two men were put back into the car, and then Mitchell punched a hole into its gas tank. Gasoline began leaking out onto the concrete floor, but some tin cans they found in the building allowed him to catch more than a gallon of it. He poured all he could into the interior of the car and over the bodies, and then they drove their own car and the motorcycles out of the building. Mitchell parked his bike outside, then got off and went back in. He produced a book of matches and tossed one into the spreading pool of gasoline. Moments later, the car was engulfed in flames.

"Let's get back to Bangkok and get the rest of our gear,"

Noah said, "and then we'll head for Pattaya. That will put us closer to the island, but not too far from our station in Bangkok."

"I can go you one better," Jenny said. "I know our station chief in Pattaya, and she happens to owe me a favor."

Noah nodded. "Then you ought to let her know we're coming, and might need to collect on it. Everybody ready?"

Everyone agreed that they were, but Neil raised a hand. Noah looked at him. "Yes?"

"I was just wondering," Neil said, "but considering it's past noon and we'll be spending God knows how long on surveillance and planning, do you think we can stop and get lunch somewhere?"

* * *

It was getting hot in the box. The wood they were built from was dark brown, nearly black, and soaked up the heat of the afternoon sun even though the air temperature was slightly below seventy degrees. Both Sarah and Sharon were soaked in their own sweat, but it failed to cool them at all because there was no breeze that could reach them.

"Kayla?" Sharon called weakly. "I don't know how much longer I can take this."

"You can take it," Sarah said. "Just try to think about someplace cool, that'll help. Just hang in there."

"No, that's not what I mean," Sharon said. "Yeah, it's hot, but that's making me need to go! I'm gonna pee myself if I don't get out of here soon."

Sarah chuckled softly. "Don't feel bad," she said. "I'm afraid I already went. If you sort of settle in the lowest corner it'll run out through the cracks onto the ground."

Sharon laughed, but there was something sarcastic about it. "How terrible is it that we even think about such things? You know how hard it is to balance in that position?"

"Yeah, but when it's either that or pee your pants, you'll find a way. I'm a lot more worried about how thirsty I'm getting than how bad this box is gonna smell by tomorrow."

"You think it'll be that long before they let us out?"

"According to some of the training I had, if you want to break someone you have to dehumanize them, make them feel like animals. That's the whole purpose of putting us in a box like this, to take away our dignity. They'll probably keep us here until we agree to whatever perversions they want us to put up with."

Sharon was quiet for a moment, but then Sarah heard her sigh. "Well, that feels a little better. So, what happens when they start making demands? Do we give in?"

"I'm not going to give in right away. To be honest, I'm holding out hope that Noah is already on the way to get us, and I'd prefer to be able to look him in the eye and say nothing happened." She bit her bottom lip for a moment before continuing. "On the other hand, staying in this box for more than a day or so will start to take its toll on us, and I mean physically as well as mentally. If you reach a point you feel you just can't take it anymore, then we'll— we'll do whatever we have to do."

When Sharon spoke again, Sarah could hear the tears in her voice. "What you're saying is that if I give in, you will, too. Right?"

Sarah smiled and tried to let the girl hear it. "Well, I can't let you get too far away from me, so where you go, I go."

Another soft sob came out of Sharon's box. "Don't worry," she said. "I won't give in if I can possibly resist. I'm just praying your Noah is as good as you say."

Sarah's smile got a little wider. "He is."

TWENTY

U nwilling to waste a lot of time, Noah had insisted that they simply grab takeout on the way back to their hotel. They ate quickly while they packed, loading all of the luggage and equipment into the trunk of the rental car, and then Noah and Jenny checked out. It was nearing four o'clock in the afternoon when they pulled out, but they had to stop for gas before they left Bangkok. Four motorcycles and a Toyota made an interesting convoy, but no one seemed to pay a whole lot of attention.

The highway to Pattaya was surprisingly busy with traffic, so the trip ended up taking a little longer than usual. They pulled up to the Budsaba Resort Hotel, where Neil had hastily arranged rooms, at just after seven, and checked in quickly. There was a restaurant attached to the resort, and they gathered there for dinner just a half-hour later.

"Pretty much everybody here speaks at least some English," Noah said, "so let's be careful what we talk about when any of the staff is within earshot. Neil, how far is it to the island from here?"

"We're only about three kilometers from the beach, and there is a place there where we can rent a fair-sized speedboat, big enough for all of us but not so big we have to hire a captain. I figured you can handle just about any boat you want to, so it seemed like the way to go. The island is about twenty kilometers away as the crow flies, and while tourists aren't allowed on the island itself, I gather it's not uncommon to go scuba diving or snorkeling up close to it. I figured that might be a good cover, don't you think?"

"That's perfect," Jenny said. "I love scuba diving. Some of us can put on a show, just in case someone on the island is watching, and maybe one or two of you can do a quick recon."

Noah nodded his head. "Marco and I will do that," he said. "It's too late to try it today, but I want to be out on the boat as early as possible. Can we rent it online?"

"No," Neil said, "'Fraid not. We have to go to the place and show ID, all the normal stuff, but it shouldn't take more than an hour or so. They open at eight, so we can be on the water by nine and at the island by ten or so."

Noah turned to Marco. "We'll be in stealth mode," he said. "Scuba to the island, then find somewhere to stash the gear while we do a deep recon. If Sarah and the target are there, we want full tactical intelligence, but we won't make a move unless the opportunity is just too good to pass up. The last thing we want to do is alert these people that we're coming, so that means no confrontations."

Marco nodded his head. "I'm with you. We go in, we snoop around, determine what the obstacles are on the path to retrieving these girls and then we get out. Plan our next move after that, right?"

"The boys and I will play in the water," Jenny said. "Be nice if we had another girl or two with us, that would look even better. Mind if I round up a couple?"

Noah nodded. "Go for it, if you can. I'd say there's a good

chance the people on the island are going to be watching any boat that comes close. If it looks like a party going on, they won't be as likely to suspect what we're really up to."

Jenny grinned and took out her phone. She poked her thumb at it a few times, then put it to her ear. "Maggie? Hey, it's Jenny. Yeah, I'm back in town, and I remember we promised to get together next time. Well, I've been invited out on a boat tomorrow for an all-day swim-and-snorkel party, but I'm gonna be the only girl with half-a-dozen guys. I thought maybe you could round up a friend and come along, help me even the odds out a little bit. Yeah, great! Okay, we'll pick you up about 7:30 in the morning. Oh, I can't wait to see you again. Wear your sexiest bikinis, and don't forget the sunscreen!"

She ended the call and looked at Noah. "Maggie's the station chief here," she said. "She'll bring one of the girls from her office to help us round out the group." She looked over at Neil. "Can we rent the scuba gear at the same place?"

"Yep," Neil said. "They even sell swimsuits there, for those of us who didn't bring any along."

Jenny gave him an odd look. "You don't pack a pair of trunks when you come out on a mission? What's wrong with you, boy?"

* * *

It was getting dark outside, but the darkness had already settled into the boxes. Both Sarah and Sharon had drifted in and out of sleep, lulled into it by the late afternoon heat that built up. Sarah couldn't guess how hot she had gotten, but it was hot enough to make her head swim.

Once, during the day, she was sure she had heard a helicopter approaching the island and landing, but she didn't recall hearing it leave again. That could mean it was still there, or that she had simply slept through its departure. When you're hot enough to be woozy, it's easy to miss out on a few details of what's going on.

Peeking through a crack in the boards, she could barely discern the glow of sunset in the distance. Just enough light came through the trees for her to see that it had a reddish glow, but she couldn't really detect shadows anymore. She had tried to be careful throughout the day, only talking to Sharon when she was fairly sure no one else was hereby, but it was always possible someone could approach them quietly enough that she wouldn't hear.

"Sharon?" Sarah called softly.

"I'm here," the girl answered. "Think it'll cool off any, with the sun going down?"

"Yeah, it'll get cooler before long. Probably cooler than we like, to be honest. I just wondered how you're holding up, you doing okay over there?"

"Not really. My back is cramping, and so are my calves. My butt feels like I've been sitting on sharp rocks all day. How about you?"

"It's definitely not comfortable in here," Sarah said with a derisive chuckle. "Did you hear a helicopter a while ago?"

"Yeah, I did. I was hoping it was your Noah, but I guess it wasn't."

"No, I guess not. Did you hear it fly away? I think I dozed off, so I don't know if it's still here or not."

"Yeah, couple hours ago. Seemed like it went off in the same direction it came from. Is that important?"

"Not really, I guess. I just wish there was some way for me to let Noah know that these people have access to a helicopter. This is obviously some kind of organized crime operation, but it would really suck if he comes to get us and they can call in reinforcements by air."

Sharon was quiet for a moment, then asked, "Do you really think he'll come?"

Sarah sighed. "He has to," she said. "You are the mission, and he can't go back without you. Failure is not a word in his vocabulary. He'll be here, there's no doubt about that."

"But how could he even find us? Somehow I doubt anyone is going to volunteer the information about where we've been taken."

"They will by the time he gets done with them," Sarah said. "This is kind of a terrible thing to say, that people like us don't worry about stuff like the Geneva Convention. If he wants to know something, somebody's going to tell him."

Sharon mulled that over for a moment. "That's kind of scary," he said. "What are you, like CIA or something?"

"No, I told you," Sarah replied. "We're the people the CIA calls when they have a problem and need someone to deal with it."

The two of them fell silent for a bit after that, as the darkness settled in. No one had even bothered to check on them since they had been locked in that morning, so Sarah assumed they would be spending the night in the boxes. She twisted herself around to get as comfortable as she could, and tried to get back to sleep.

The heat in the box gradually lulled her to sleep, but it was fitful. She woke and dozed off several times before the dawn began to show through the cracks.

"You awake?" Sharon asked as the light spread slowly across the clearing.

"I am," Sarah said. "Did you get any sleep at all?"

"Off and on. This isn't exactly the most comfortable place I've ever tried to spend the night. Think anybody will even check on us today?"

"Yeah. They know we are hungry and thirsty and extremely uncomfortable in other ways. I think it's time to start making their demands."

Sharon groaned as she tried to twist herself into a more comfortable position. "If they'd just give us something to drink, some water or something. I'm hungry, but I can cope with that. It's the thirst that's driving me crazy."

"I know what you mean. I don't think my throat's been this dry in years." She hesitated for a moment, wishing they could see each other. "Sharon, if you don't feel like you can hold out any longer..."

"I'm not to that point yet," Sharon said. "I'm just worried about how soon they're going to take the choice away from us."

Sarah nodded, even though Sharon couldn't see it. "I understand. I'm still hoping Noah will show up before it gets to that point."

"Yeah. I hope so too."

* * *

"Noah," Jenny said, "this is Maggie."

Noah shook hands with the pretty brunette. "Thanks for your help," he said.

Maggie smiled and nodded. "Not a problem," she said. She turned and nodded her head toward the girl beside her. "This is Julie. She's my liaison with the embassy. Don't worry, she's cleared."

Noah shook Julie's hand. "I gather you both know

Jenny," he said. "I'm Noah, and the rest of this crowd is Neil, Marco, Jim, Dave and Randy. Neil and Marco are with me, the rest of these guys work with Jenny."

Julie smiled. "I've met Jenny's boys before, but it's a pleasure to meet Team Camelot. You guys are something of a legend."

Jenny backhanded Noah on his arm. "That sucks," she said. "I've been at this a year longer than you have, and nobody calls me a legend."

"I think," Neil said, "that has something to do with the fact that Noah is known for walking into deadly traps and turning them around on his enemies. I saw him carry explosives right into one of those traps and set them off in the bad guy's face. He ain't a guy you want for an enemy, trust me on that."

"Well, there's that, I guess," Jenny said, "but some of us are smarter than that. The only trap I plan to walk into is the one I'm setting for somebody else."

"Legends are nothing but conceit that's bestowed on you by someone else," Noah said. "I just do my job. For today, that means putting on a show to distract any guards that might be watching from the island. You three girls can play with the rest of these guys and make it as realistic as possible. While you're doing that, Marco and I are going to be crawling the floor of the bay until we reach a spot on the shore that will let us get into the jungle. My target and one of my team are supposedly being held on that island, and I intend to get them back."

Maggie grinned at him. "That's another part of the legend," she said. "Your girl keeps getting in trouble, and you keep risking her neck to get her out."

"Team Camelot doesn't leave anyone behind," Neil said. "He's risked his life for me and..." His voice trailed off.

"So I've heard. That's why we're glad we can help, this time. Neither of us was chosen for fieldwork, so we are more than happy to get a little shot at it."

"All right, then let's go," Noah said. Maggie and Julie followed them to where the car and motorcycles were parked, and each of the girls climbed onto the back of a bike. Maggie rode with Jim, while Julie climbed on behind Randy. Jenny laughed at the two of them, then deliberately climbed on the back of Noah's bike. "Just pretend I'm your girlfriend," she whispered into his ear.

Noah said nothing, but started the bike and put it in gear. Dave and Neil rode in the car, and all four of the motorcycles followed them to the boat rental facility.

The next ninety minutes was taken up with paperwork and credit cards, but finally they were able to load a dozen sets of scuba gear and a cooler full of beer and sandwiches onto the thirty-six-foot cabin cruiser Noah had selected. He fired up the big Yanmar diesel engine and eased the boat out of its slip and into the bay. Once they were out of the low-speed area, he pointed the boat to the southwest and shoved the throttle forward.

"We should have brought skis," Jenny yelled over the wind and the roar of the engine, standing beside him. "I love skiing."

"You act like you're on vacation," Neil said. "Do you ever get serious?"

Jim Marino clapped him on the shoulder. "You watched her interrogate those guys yesterday, and you can still ask that question? Trust me, she'll be plenty serious when it comes time to make our move."

Neil glared at him, but said nothing.

The boat made pretty good time, and they dropped anchor just to the northeast of the island less than forty minutes later. They spent half an hour just wandering back and forth from the cabin to the deck, trying to confuse any observers as to how many people were actually on the boat. Then, Noah, Marco, Randy, Jenny and Julie all donned scuba gear and fell backward into the water from the far side of the vessel. They stayed under for a bit, while Neil, Maggie, Jim and Dave made a show of sunbathing on the deck, but then the two girls climbed back aboard. They dropped their gear at the stern, and shoved the guys over so they could lay out in the sun with Maggie.

Randy and Jim would surface occasionally, usually tossing something up onto the deck. They would call back and forth to those on board about the undersea treasures they were hoping to find, then dive again. At other times, the girls would stand up and call down to the surface on the far side of the boat, as if they were talking to the other divers.

The act wasn't wasted. Just inside the tree line on the shore, two men stood and watched through binoculars. After an hour of watching the divers playing around, they found themselves paying more attention to the three bikini-clad beauties than to any activity in the water.

TWENTY-ONE

Noah and Marco had popped up near the boat a couple of times in the first minutes after they had all dived in, but then they went down to fifteen feet and started toward the eastern side of the island. Neil had shown them a Google Earth image of the island that indicated a heliport on that side, along with areas that might be more easily accessible to people on foot. Noah was guessing that this area would be the most likely choice for the type of camp the Nay Thas would operate from.

Fortunately, the angle of the sun to the water made it nearly impossible for anyone on the island shoreline to see below the surface. Since both of them were skilled scuba divers, they were able to maintain steady motion without a great deal of exertion. With two aluminum-80 tanks each, they had no trouble swimming just under half a kilometer to get to the area Noah had chosen for their landing.

As soon as they were out of view from the boat, they made their way to the white sand beach. The spot Noah had selected was one of the narrowest beaches on the island, and it took them only a few seconds to jog from the water into the tree line. They stashed the scuba gear in some of the scrub, and Noah opened the waterproof bag he had towed along with him and removed his cell phone, along with the tracking sensors and tablet they had used to keep track of Sarah in the prison.

He set the first of the sensors in the crook of a tree, high enough to be out of sight of anyone walking by, then handed one to Marco and pointed off to the west, while he took the third and started south. Fifteen minutes later, he turned on the tablet as he returned to their starting point, and showed it to Marco.

The red dot that indicated Sarah was nearby was blinking steadily. "She's here," he said. "From the map Neil made on this thing, I'd say she's about three hundred yards in that direction." He pointed to the southwest. He shut down the tablet and hid it with the other gear, and then he and Marco began moving quietly toward the lower areas of the island.

They'd gone only a few hundred feet when they saw the first armed man. He was leaning against a tree, smoking a cigarette and paying no attention to his surroundings. Noah froze and watched as the man finished his smoke, then stretched and walked further into the woods to the south. Marco, behind him, waited until the man was out of sight before moving carefully up beside his boss.

"Definitely something going on here," he whispered.

"Something that seems to require guards with assault rifles," Noah replied. "Let's try to get closer to where he was headed."

Still moving stealthily, the two of them slowly advanced in the same direction the armed man had gone. He seemed to have been on patrol, making a circuit around the area and watching for possible intruders, but he seemed rather lax in his attention to detail. Moving parallel to the path he had taken, Noah spotted a number of cigarette butts that indicated the fellow came this way often.

The circuitous route they had taken covered nearly half a mile by the time they saw the simple, rugged huts of the main compound. There were only six of them, and two of them were considerably larger than the others. Noah and Marco moved carefully around the area, and Noah snapped several photos with his phone. The zoom feature let him look closely at the dozen or so women in the compound, and he was disappointed that he didn't see Sarah or Sharon Ingersoll.

He also saw numerous men with weapons, estimating there were at least a couple dozen of them. Only one or two had sidearms, while the rest carried Kalashnikov AK-74s, a later version of the famous AK-47 that had been the foundation of so many assault rifles developed over the last sixty-five years.

Keeping a careful watch, they slowly made their way around the opposite side, and that was when Marco caught a glimpse of the isolation boxes. There were ten of them, cubes about four feet on a side. Two of them were closed, and each of those had a pin in the hasp to keep the lid secure.

The clearing around the boxes made it impossible to approach them without being seen from the path that led to the compound, so Noah continued moving through the trees behind them. When he was confident that one of the closed boxes was between him and the opening of the path, he picked up a small pebble and threw it at the box.

There was no reaction at first, so he picked up a second and threw it. A second later, he could hear motion inside the box.

Very carefully, Noah moved forward until his face was just outside of the shadow of the trees above. A gasp from inside the box make him draw back quickly, but there was no further sound. He and Marco froze and watched for a moment, and his caution was rewarded.

"Sharon? You awake?" Sarah's voice came softly to Noah's ears.

"Yeah," said another voice from the other box. "And thirsty and miserable and I wish to God I'd never even heard of Thailand."

"Well, I can't help you with that," Sarah said, "but you might try having a little faith in my guys. I'm pretty sure they're getting close, and probably planning what to do about us even now."

"That's what you keep saying," Sharon said, "but I sure wish they'd come pretty soon. I'm not sure I can hold out a lot longer."

Noah flicked another pebble at the box Sarah was in. "Hang in there, kiddo," she said. "I promise you, it won't be a lot longer. Noah will probably be here by tonight. We can last that long, right?"

Something in Sarah's voice seemed to reach the other girl. "You really think so?" she asked. "God, I hope you're right."

Sarah chuckled. "Yep. Pretty sure I am. Just hang in there with me, okay?"

Noah moved further back into the denser brush, and then he and Marco started moving on around the site. Forty minutes later, they arrived back at their gear and slipped into their tank harnesses. A careful scan of the beach revealed no obvious surveillance, so they hurried into the water and slipped under the waves again.

The return trip took even less time than the one from the boat, simply because an underwater current seemed to move them along in the right direction. They swam in under the boat and caught sight of Neil, Randy, Jenny and the other two girls swimming and splashing on the surface, while Jim and Dave were still leisurely diving along the coral reef. Noah and Marco joined them for a few minutes, and then Noah signaled Marco to go aboard while he and the others stayed below.

Ten minutes later, Noah climbed onto the boat and dropped his tanks with other discarded ones at the stern, and then went below into the cabin. He lay down on one of the couches and closed his eyes, taking the opportunity to get a little rest while he could.

A part of his mind was planning the attack he would lead on the island later that night, but another part was just thinking of Sarah. Without even realizing it, Noah was clenching the fist he planned to use on whoever had put her into that box. He let himself remember their last hour alone at home, when she had accepted his proposal, and the barest hint of a smile turned up the edges of his mouth as he drifted off to sleep.

An hour later, after everyone else had climbed aboard, Neil gently shook him awake. "Hey, Boss? It's almost two o'clock. Think we ought to be heading back?"

Noah came awake instantly. "Yes. We're going to need another boat for tonight, though. Something less flashy and a lot quieter. I want to make landfall as silently as possible tonight, but it's got to be big enough to take us all. Any ideas?"

Neil grinned at him. "Just let me get online, and I'll find something. I take it you found her? Them, I mean?"

Noah nodded. "Yes," he said. "They're alive, going

through the breaking process. Sarah's holding up, and keeping the other girl from giving up."

"Good," Neil said, and Noah noticed the moisture in his eyes. "Then we're going in tonight, to get them out, right?"

"Yes. I'll take Jenny and the others, while you—"

"Don't leave me out, Noah," Neil said suddenly, and there was a pleading sound in his voice. "I can handle it, just give me my Uzi. This is Sarah we're talking about, don't leave me behind, please?"

Noah looked him in the eye. "I was about to say that I'd take the others in with me, while you stand guard at the boat. If anyone comes near you without signaling that it's one of us, you fire. Got it?"

The tall, skinny kid looked down at Noah and smiled his widest. "I got it," he said, and then he dragged an arm across his eyes quickly. "I won't let you down."

Noah put a hand on his shoulder. "I know," he said, then went topside and started the engine. The rest of the group continued to put on the party act until they were well away from the island once again, and then Jenny sidled up to Noah.

"Marco says they're there?" she asked.

Noah nodded. "Yes. I counted about two dozen armed guards. We're going in tonight, after dark. Neil thinks he can find us a quiet boat, so we'll hit them hard and fast. I want to be in and out before they get a chance to call for help."

"Good," Jenny said with a grin. "Kill 'em all and let God sort 'em out?"

Noah stared out over the water as he nodded once again. "Exactly," he said.

* * *

He's here! Sarah thought. *He's found us! Oh, if only there was a way I could tell Sharon without giving him away.*

She'd known he would come, of course. The one thing she was absolutely certain of was that Noah would never abandon her to her fate. As long as she was alive, he would do whatever it took to get her back. That was why she had told Sharon over and over that all they had to do was survive.

From the shadows she had been able to see through the crack in the boards, it had been close to noon when he had appeared in the woods behind her. The first time the pebble had hit the box she had been dozing off, but then it had come again. Without even suspecting that Noah might have been behind it, she had twisted around and peeked through a crack to see what might be back there causing things to hit the box, and that was the precise moment when he had leaned forward and let the sunlight hit his face.

Her heart had leapt into her throat, just from the sight of him. She understood perfectly why he didn't make a move to rescue her at that time, but she knew he'd be back. He would have been doing reconnaissance this time, getting the lay of the land and finding out how many guards there might be. If she knew him—and she did—he'd be back for her when the sun went down.

She had encouraged Sharon the best she could, but she didn't dare say out loud that she had seen him. If one of the guards overheard, they would be on the watch for him, and it suddenly dawned on her that she had already said far too much. She had openly talked about her hope of rescue, and that he would be coming for them. She can only pray now that the guards had not overheard, or at least had not understood her words.

Suddenly, the sound of a helicopter rattled overhead, and she hoped and prayed that Noah was off the island and far enough away to avoid its notice. Could it be that he had been spotted, and that reinforcements had been called in as she had feared?

No, she didn't think so. This would probably be about the same time they had heard the helicopter the day before, so it was more likely that it was a daily supply run of some sort. She continued to tell herself that, because the possibility that Noah had been captured was simply unbearable.

That thought only strengthened her resolve not to risk exposing him in the future. She tried to think of a way to warn Sharon not to mention him anymore, but even that could give him away. From that moment on, she told herself, any conversation between the two of them would leave Noah completely out of it. The most she could do would be to simply encourage the other girl not to give up.

Even as these thoughts went through her mind, she heard the crunching of brush and twigs that meant one of the guards was coming their way. She leaned forward and peeked through a crack and saw that it was Cho, the one who had put them in the boxes the day before. It had been more than twenty-four hours since that time, and she had wondered when someone would come to see if it was long enough.

The pin was removed from her hasp, and bright sunlight blinded her for a moment when the lid was thrown open. Rough hands reached in and grabbed her by one arm and her hair, and she struggled to get to her feet before she was yanked bald.

"Hey!" she yelled. "Take it easy!"

One of those rough hands slapped her across the face, and she felt as if her head had been knocked loose. A wave of dizziness and nausea swept over her, but she clamped her mouth shut and managed not to throw up.

The hand holding her hair let go, and slid between her legs to lift her over the side of the box. The indignity of the contact struck her, but she was more concerned with what might be coming next.

Cho set her on her feet and shook her a couple of times, apparently trying to make her stand on her own. She managed to open her eyes and saw two other men approaching her. One of them was Pak, still dressed in something like combat fatigues as he had been the day before, but the other man wore a business suit.

TWENTY-TWO

"**S**top your struggling, little flower," Pak said. "Mr. Lom has come to see you. Stand straight, so that he may see your virtues."

"Screw you," Sarah said. "The least you could do is let a girl take a shower and clean up before you try to show her off."

Pak smiled at her. "Cleanliness, or the lack of it, is not a factor. Mr. Lom is seeking a western girl who might entertain some of his clientele. His tastes, and theirs, demand the girl be full of spirit, but not that she be washed and perfumed."

The business suit said something in Thai, and Pak responded in the same language. He twirled his finger in the air, and Cho spun her around so that she could be seen from the back. A moment later, she was turned round again, and this time Cho reached up and ripped the prison shirt down its front with one hand.

Her bra had been taken at the prison, so she instinctively tried to cover herself. Her hands were roughly yanked away, and a warning slap conveyed the message that she should not try it again. She forced herself to stand straight despite having her breasts on display, and looked a morning challenge into the eye of the business suit.

Lom spoke again, and then reached inside his jacket. His hand reappeared holding a large sheaf of money, which he passed to Pak.

"I was correct," Pak said. "You are precisely what he was looking for. It is a pity that his purchases do not last long. But of course, that is why your price is greater than you would bring in ten years as a bar girl."

Sarah turned and stared at him, and her eyes grew wide. "You think you can sell me?" she demanded. "Are you insane?"

Pak burst out laughing. "I assure you, little flower, I am quite sane. As I told you before, I am a man who enjoys wealth and power. I achieve both by providing such men with the entertainments they desire."

Inside, Sarah was panicking. How could this be happening now? She had seen Noah, she knew that he was coming to get her, but this monster wanted to take her away? How would he ever find her again?

Cho took hold of the back of her neck, as Lom turned and started walking back down the path. With him pushing her along, Sarah had no choice but to follow, but she was determined not to make it easy. Before they had gone five steps, she managed to twist her left leg around and kick her captor in his groin.

Cho instantly let go of her, and she turned toward the man who had just bought her. His eyes were wide, but there was a strange smile on his face as she spun a roundhouse kick that caught him squarely on his left ear. The smile vanished and was replaced with a look of utter surprise as he fell, but then something struck the back of her head.

She managed not to fall and spun to see what had

happened, and saw that Pak had attacked her while she was distracted. His stance indicated training in the martial arts, but Sarah had been through some pretty intense training of her own. She snapped into position and waited for his next attack, which came almost instantly.

She managed to duck the punch he swung at her face, and drove her foot into his solar plexus as he spun past her. He managed to remain on his feet, but he was gasping for breath as he turned to face her again.

"Come on, you piece of crap," she said. "Come on, let's see what you got!"

A sudden shout from Sharon's box caused her to glance toward it, and then the lights went out as Cho wrapped his arm around her throat and squeezed. It was a classic sleeper hold, and she was unconscious within seconds.

Pak helped his customer get back to his feet, profusely apologizing for the rebellious acts of the stupid girl. Lom brushed off his apologies and simply asked him to have her brought to the helicopter. Pak instantly agreed, and shouted for a couple of other men. With Cho, they bound her hands and feet and then she was thrown over the shoulder of one of them and carried down the path.

Lom began to follow, with Pak beside him. In Thai, and watching Pak from the corner of his eye, Lom said, "This one has more spirit. Perhaps she will not die so quickly."

Pak smiled. "My old friend, you cannot expect such delicate flowers to endure the storms to which you subject them without being damaged. If you would keep her in your service, you must caution your clients to keep themselves under control. Exercising their passions is her purpose, but that does not mean that they should not leave her able to recover."

"There are only a few who go to such extremes. I have

long thought that there might be a girl somewhere who could defend herself against them. Perhaps this is the one." He grinned slightly at Pak. "Of course, if this proves to be the case, you may not earn so much money this year. So far, I have bought one girl each month. This one could surprise us and last much longer."

Ahead of them, Sarah had awakened and begun loudly cursing the man who was carrying her. She was thrashing about and doing her best to kick him or strike him with an elbow, until he finally threw her to the ground. A single kick to the side of her head put a stop to her resistance, and Pak watched as the man who had kicked her bent down and looked closely at her, then put a hand to her throat and scowled.

Pak rolled his eyes to Lom. "She will not last the day, if she continues to antagonize my men. You do recall, I'm sure, that all sales are final."

* * *

Sharon heard the loud *clunk* as Sarah's box was thrown open, and pressed her eye to one of the cracks in her own. She saw Cho drag Sarah out of the box, and then moved to another crack when she heard Pak speak.

It took only a second for her to understand what was happening, and she nearly panicked when she realized that Sarah was being taken away, was actually being sold as if she were nothing more than a piece of property. What would she do if Sarah were gone? Up until now, she had barely let herself hope that the mythical Noah would truly appear, and while Sarah insisted that Sharon was the true objective of any such rescue, her only real confidence rested in the hope that he would come for the girl who was one of his own.

And then Sarah was fighting, putting two of the men on the ground before they even seemed to realize it. Sharon's heart rushed into her throat as she watched through the gap, but then Cho got back to his feet and it was Sarah who went down, obviously unconscious. Pak called for someone, and Sarah was quickly bound and carried away.

Alone, Sharon quickly felt her last vestiges of hope slipping away. Sarah had told her to survive, but she wondered now if that would even be possible.

The tears started to fall before she even realized she was crying. They were the tears of despair that come from someone who has lost all hope.

* * *

By the time they got back to the rental facility, Neil had already come up with a game plan. "Look at this," he said to Noah as he steered the boat home. He turned the computer so that Noah could see the screen, and pointed at the deep vee-hulled boat that occupied its center. "This baby is a forty-four footer, and it has an electric inboard motor that runs on thirty deep-cycle twelve-volt batteries. It can make its maximum speed of eight knots for up to five hours on a charge, and there's a generator on board in case you need it. It's actually built for deep-sea fishing in environmentally sensitive areas, places where the loud noise of a gas or diesel engine might be prohibited, but it's ideal for our purpose. In the dark, with all of us down low behind the gunwales, it should be just about impossible for anyone to know we're coming."

"That looks good," Noah said. "Where do we get it?"

Neil grinned. "Actually, we just bought it. This is a used one that was up for sale, so I got Maggie and Julie to help me set up a dummy Thai Corporation, and we bought it through the business. We bought our own boathouse and pier, too, because it was sort of a package deal. It was a tourist fishing outfit that was going out of business."

Noah looked up at him. "I don't suppose you bothered to get Allison's authorization to spend that much money?"

"Actually, no," Neil said. "But that's because I didn't spend any money. I did a ghost transfer into the new corporate account, used that to buy everything. Now in about four days, somebody's going to get all upset when all that money vanishes, but none of it can lead back to any of us. We'll let the Thai authorities try to figure out who the boat and boathouse belong to after that, right?"

Noah raised one eyebrow in what Neil thought of as the closest thing he ever did to smiling. It was a gesture of approval, and Neil was always happy when he saw it.

"Where is the boat house," Noah asked, "and how long will it take us to get from there to the island?"

"That's the best part," Neil said with a big grin. "It's just north of the village of Hat So, which is about two miles across the channel from your chosen landing site. The boat is already there, and the previous owner has agreed to wait and show us around this evening. He is expecting us this afternoon, but he thinks we're just employees of the corporation. It turns out Julie speaks fluent Thai, so she made the phone calls. She told him that she is sending a bunch of Americans who have experience in running such a business to take it over for her."

Noah turned his attention back to the bay, steering the boat toward its dock. "That's some excellent planning, Neil," he said. "I'll make a point of telling Allison just how excellent it was when we get back."

Turning the boat back in took a bit of time, but the boat

yard's crew took care of unloading all the scuba gear and cleaning it up. A short time later, they dropped off Maggie and Julie at Maggie's place, and picked up an extra headset for Jenny from Maggie's equipment room. After that, they grabbed a quick dinner and were on the way south, once again on Highway 3, by five o'clock.

The drive to Hat So took almost 20 minutes, mostly because of the smaller roads they had to follow once they left the highway. It was just after six o'clock by the time they arrived at the boathouse, and Mr. Loy, the former owner, was waiting in the office to greet them.

Mr. Loy spoke very little English, but was able to convey the gist of what he wanted to say about how he had run the business up to that point. It had been a one-man operation, with Loy himself acting as manager and captain of the boat. He explained that he would run the generator to power the boat until he got close to the coral reefs around Khram Yai island, then shut it down and run on the electric motors in compliance with noise and pollution restrictions imposed by the Royal Thai Navy. The fishing in those waters was excellent, he said, but only silent fishing vessels were allowed to operate so close to the coral.

Showing them how to operate the boat took only a few minutes, and he pronounced himself satisfied with the way Noah handled it in the test run. The boat was essentially nothing but a long hull with a control panel and tiller at the stern, and padded benches that ran the length of the vessel on each side. Fishermen, he explained, would either sit or kneel on the benches as they cast their lines into the water. The batteries were mounted along the keel, putting all the weight at the very bottom.

Loy was gone by ten o'clock, and the two teams began loading their weapons into the boat. Noah said he wanted to wait until just past midnight to start toward the island, letting the guards and any other personnel at the compound get as relaxed as possible before their assault. He knew from his military experience that midnight truly is the witching hour, the time when soldiers and others on duty begin to think more about how soon their shift will end than what their responsibilities might be.

"Here's the plan, the way I've got it figured out," he said. "The way this boat is built, we can drive it right into the beach. Jenny, your team will move in just to the north of the compound, while Marco and I will head directly to the isolation boxes. We'll be using the headsets for direct communication, but I want to maintain radio silence until the fireworks began. If Sarah and Sharon are still in the isolation boxes, we'll do our best to get them out silently. If not, then Marco and I will begin a full-frontal assault. As soon as that happens, Jenny, I want you and your team to move in."

"Slice and dice, right?" Jenny asked. "Any of them that are armed are targets. I was thinking, though, that we don't want to kill everyone until we have both the girls. If for any reason we don't find them, I'll need someone to interrogate."

"Good point," Noah said. "We'll make landfall just about the same place where Marco and I did earlier today, and the tablet is stashed near there. It should give us a good idea of where Sarah is, and hopefully Sharon will still be with her. If not, we'll grab Sarah and hope that she can tell us where to find Ms. Ingersoll. Barring that, we'll just search the whole island if we have to."

"Aww," Jenny said, "but interrogation is so much more fun!"

Neil rolled his eyes. "You're just evil, you know that?"

Jenny blinked at him. "Of course I am, sweetheart, that's why they pay me the big bucks."

Marco nudged Neil with an elbow. "She has a point," he said.

Neil insisted that he was hungry, so he and Dave ran out to try to find sandwiches. They had to drive quite some distance to find an open door, but came back a bit later with sliced pork and unsliced bread. Marco managed to do a fair job of cutting the bread with a dive knife he had acquired earlier, and they all sat down to eat before launching the boat on its mission of murder and mayhem.

TWENTY-THREE

Darkness had fallen, and Sharon was feeling more alone than ever. The sun had not been down long, she knew, but the dark seemed so oppressive that it almost made her breathing difficult. She kept hoping that Sarah would return, but the later it got, the less she believed it would happen.

She heard footsteps crunching toward her, and then the top of her box was thrown open. She looked up into the face of a man she hadn't seen before, and he grinned at her.

"You want out?" he asked her.

Terrified of what was coming next, Sharon tried hard to decline, but she heard her own voice say, "Oh, please, please let me out, please, I can't take…"

The man reached in and took hold of her arm. At first he seemed gentle, as he helped her rise to her feet, but then he simply leaned into her and dragged her over the top of the box on his shoulder. He dropped her onto her feet, but her legs had been cramped up too long and collapsed. She sat down hard, and the man looked down at her and laughed. "You fall down," he said. "You in good position, and you ready to be whore?"

Tears began flowing down her face as she shook her

head, and once again she heard her voice begging. "Please, please, no, please..."

Still laughing, the man grabbed her hair and dragged her to her feet once more. "You stink," he said. "You make mess on you self, you need bath." He turned her around and started marching her along the path, continuing until they entered the compound. He walked her to a short, round structure, and when he suddenly picked her up and threw her in, she realized that it was a large vat of water.

The water was cold and closed over her head, but she came up a moment later gasping for breath. The man was laughing again, and she suddenly realized that they were surrounded by a few other men and numerous women. The women were chuckling at her, while the men were simply standing there and staring.

She spit out water that had gotten into her mouth, and the taste told her that this was bathwater. There was a soapy flavor, and that was explained a moment later when the man who had pitched her in reached in and grabbed a bar of soap that was floating on the surface and brandished it at her. "You wash," he said. "You wash now. We no like stinky whore."

Surrounded as she was, Sharon didn't dare refuse. She took the soap and began rubbing it onto her hands and face, but the man suddenly grabbed her hair and pulled her toward him once more. "Take off clothes," he yelled at her. "You take bath, no clothes!"

Crying her heart out, Sharon began removing her clothing. The loose prison shirt came off over her head, and she sank low to keep her breasts under the water as she took off her pants. She instinctively tossed both of them onto the edge of the makeshift tub, and some of the women grabbed them and took them away.

Sharon picked up the soap again, and turned around, trying to find a way to wash modestly, but there were men watching from every direction. At last, she took a deep breath and remembered that Sarah had told her it was necessary to do whatever it took to survive, so she rose onto her knees and began washing herself.

One of the other men reached in and grabbed the waist-band of her panties, and they ripped off easily. "You wash all," he said, and she steeled herself against the embar-rassment as she rose to her feet and continued to wash the rest of her body as the crowd watched.

You can do this, she told herself. *You can do this because Noah will be coming. Sarah was so certain, she had to be right. Noah must be coming, and I have to be ready when he does.*

That thought gave her strength, and she bent down and got her hair wet, then began rubbing the soap into it. She stood again, ignoring the men and women who were ogling her body as she worked up a lather in her hair, then scrubbed it into her scalp as hard as she could. Her body was on full display, she knew, but it didn't seem to matter anymore. All that mattered was survival, no matter what else might happen to her.

She dipped down to rinse herself off, then leaned against the side as she brought up her legs and washed them. The men were beginning to smile at her, and she forced herself to smile back. The looks on their faces told her what was coming, but she simply focused on the ne-cessity for her own survival.

The man who had brought her to the water began to act impatient, and she decided that it would be better to face the inevitable than try to postpone it. She dropped the soap and rinsed herself once more, then stood and faced him. She held out one hand, and his impatience turned to a smile as he took hold of it and helped her to balance as she stepped out of the tub and onto a rock.

A couple of the women came close, and dried her off with some rough towels that didn't smell as clean as she would have liked, and then a simple shift was pulled over her head. Another woman tossed a pair of simple sandals onto the rock in front of her feet, and she stepped into them, working her toes to get them situated properly.

As soon as she was dressed like all of the other women, the man who was still holding her hand tugged on it, and she was led toward one of the huts. She didn't resist as he pulled her inside, and she saw the simple, handmade bed that stood in the middle of it. He pointed, and she walked as calmly as possible to the bed and sat down on it, and that's when she realized that four other men had followed them inside.

"You take off clothes again," the first man said, and she fought back the tears that wanted to flow once more as she pulled the shirt over her head and laid it across the foot of the bed. She kicked off the sandals without being told, then lifted her legs and lay down on the rough mattress.

The man grinned, and nodded to the others. A moment later, they all stood naked around her, while the first man climbed onto the bed.

* * *

Because they wanted to be as stealthy as possible, Noah didn't bother to start the generator when they pulled away from the pier. The batteries were fully charged and capable of making it to the island and back more than once, so they ran silent. At full speed, however, the boat made a loud rustling sound as it passed through the water, so he cut the speed down to three knots when they got within a half-mile of the island.

With no lights, and only a sliver of a moon above them, the boat was essentially invisible. He ran the boat aground on the same beach where he and Marco had swum ashore earlier in the day, and they left Neil to guard the vessel as the rest of them disembarked. They entered the trees and found the waterproof bag Noah had hidden earlier, and he quickly withdrew the tablet and powered it on.

"She's not showing up," he said. "I suppose it's possible the tracker has failed, or it may have been broken if she's been manhandled enough. We're going to proceed on the assumption that she's here somewhere, but let's also be prepared to ask questions. She was in a hotbox earlier, and I doubt they would consider her properly broken so soon." He looked up at the others. "Also, remember that Sharon Ingersoll is the mission objective. Marco and I will check the boxes where we last had position on her, but if anyone finds her, I want you to break radio silence and let me know."

Jenny and her men moved quickly toward the north side of the compound, navigating by instinct according to the map Noah had drawn for them. Noah let them have a moment's head start, then he and Marco started toward the area where the isolation boxes had been.

As planned, there was radio silence until Noah and Marco reached the boxes. Marco made a soft clucking sound when they saw that all of the boxes were open, this time, but Noah only glanced at him. He stood and looked at the boxes for a few seconds, then spoke into the microphone beside his cheek.

"This is Camelot," he said. "Objective is at large. Report any sighting."

He looked at Marco again, and used hand signals to direct him to start through the trees along the right side of the path, while he took the left side. The main compound was only 100 yards or so away, and they moved quietly through the wooded area until it came into view.

There were three men standing in the middle of the compound, each holding an assault rifle. Noah aimed his pistol carefully, and the silencer made a *thwut* sound that reminded him of a bare foot hitting mud. The first of the three men dropped, and the silencer sounded twice more. All three of them were down on the ground, a third eye suddenly centered in their foreheads.

While the silencer's noise was not enough to rouse anyone else in the compound, the rattle of three assault rifles falling to the ground did. After a couple of seconds, a half-dozen men came stumbling sleepily out of two of the huts, while a male voice was heard demanding to know what was going on from a third.

More silencers sounded, but then there came the boom of Jenny's own pistol, a nine millimeter Beretta she had produced from the hidden compartment in one of her bags. Immediately afterward, a man began screaming, but he was drowned out by Jenny's voice.

"Oh, stop squalling," she shouted. "You didn't need that anymore, anyway." The gun boomed again, and the screaming stopped.

The third hut, where the man in charge seemed to have been hiding as he demanded information, suddenly discharged a couple more men, followed by one more man who was holding a woman in front of himself as a shield.

Noah recognized Sharon Ingersoll instantly, despite the fact that she was naked. He raised his pistol and fired once, and the man holding her developed third eye of his own.

Sharon began to scream as she was dragged to the ground, the dead man's hand still gripping her neck as he fell. Marco took out the other two, as Noah ran to Sharon and yanked her free. He started to speak to her, but an assault rifle rattled, and he felt the touch of fire as one of its bullets passed between his left arm and his ribs, digging a three-inch gouge on the inside of his arm.

He spun and fired in a single movement, keeping the girl behind his body. The man who had fired at him fell, but there were more of them coming into view. A quick scan of the area showed him seven dead bodies, but that meant there were still more than a dozen armed men he couldn't account for.

"I have the objective," he said into the headset. "Be alert for any sign of the second objective and report immediately if found."

"You're Noah," Sharon said suddenly, but other armed men were trying to take aim at them. Noah fired again in their direction, causing them to scatter for cover, while he dragged her away from the hut and toward the trees. Some of the men were trying to pursue, and he could hear the rattle of automatic fire punctuated by the loud *thwack* of bullets striking the trees around them.

"I've got you covered," Marco's voice said in his ear. An instant later, Noah heard the sound of Marco's own silencer. At least one of the men pursuing him grunted and fell, but Noah wasn't ready to turn around and look behind him. The mission objective was Sharon, and it was imperative that she survive and be evacuated as soon as possible. He kept running, dragging her along stumbling behind him, and listening to the sound of the gun battle going on behind them.

"I have located several women, but objective two is not present," said Marino through the headsets.

"I concur, objective two does not seem to be present," Lange echoed.

"Well, don't give up," Jenny said through the headsets. "I don't want to take a chance on leaving the girl behind, so let's look everywhere! Randy, you and Jim make sure you check all the huts, look anywhere she might be concealed!"

"Yes, ma'am," said Randy, and he was echoed a second later by Jim Marino.

TWENTY-FOUR

Noah pushed Sharon behind him again and fired twice more. The latest man who'd been shooting at them ducked down, and Noah could see him running away. He turned to the girl who was cowering and crying against his back.

"Where is Sarah?" He demanded, but she didn't seem to hear him at first. He grabbed her chin and tilted her face up so that she was looking at him and repeated the question. Her eyebrows drew together and she looked confused. Noah instantly realized his mistake. "Kayla," he said. "What happened to Kayla?"

"I—I don't know," she said shakily. "The men, they took her a few hours ago. There was this other man, and he gave the head guy here a bunch of money for her. I don't think she's here anymore."

Noah stared at her for a couple of seconds, then took her by the hand and began moving back toward the trees. "First thing I've got to do is get you out of here," he said. "After that, I'll find out where they took her. Marco, did you catch that?"

The earpiece came alive in his ear. "Negative, what's going on?"

"I've got Sharon, I'm getting her out. She says Sarah was

taken away some time ago, apparently sold."

"Well, crap," Marco's staticky voice said. "Sounds like we need some more intelligence, right?"

"Chill, Noah," came Jenny's voice. "Boys, keep a couple of the watchdogs alive and healthy for me. I'll find out where she's gone."

"Copy that," Noah said. "Neil, what's the situation at the boat?"

The chatter of the little Uzi sounded briefly. Neil didn't answer for a couple of seconds, but then Noah heard: "Only seen one man down here so far, and I think I just killed him. You gonna get here soon?"

"Ten minutes," Noah said. "Hold it together for me till I get there."

"I'm trying," Neil said, "but it's all I can do not to puke my guts out."

Behind him, Noah could hear the sound of Glocks mingling with the rattle of Kalashnikovs. The assault rifles were excellent weapons, but close-quarter fighting like this was better done with handguns. He had no doubt that Marco, Jenny and her team were cutting down the ranks of the *Nay Thas* soldiers.

Suddenly, the island went silent just as Noah saw the boat come into view. "Neil," he said into the headset. "I'm coming out of the woods to your left. Scan the beach, is it clear?"

"It's clear," the shaky voice replied. "Hurry up, will you? I really need to be sick."

Still holding Sharon's hand, Noah stepped out into the open and scanned around himself while making his way toward the boat. As he got close, he saw Neil lean over the far side and heard the sounds of retching. A dozen yards away, he saw the reason why.

One of the men from the compound had apparently tried to investigate the boat, but Neil had followed Noah's orders perfectly. As soon as he could clearly see that he was dealing with an armed man, he had shouted a warning. When that man aimed his rifle toward the boat, Neil had sprayed him with the little submachine gun, dropping him where he stood.

Neil understood what the team did, and was always ready to do his job—but he was simply not a killer. Had he not been certain that the other man would have killed him, Noah doubted the boy would ever have been able to pull the trigger.

The silence on the island continued for several minutes, though he could hear the chatter of the others through the headset. Marco and Randy had captured a couple of the men, and were holding them for Jenny's arrival. When she got there, all of them turned off their headsets.

It didn't make much of a difference. The first of the men began screaming only a few seconds later, and that was followed by shouting from the second. Noah couldn't make out the words, but he was quite sure they were being spoken in answer to the questions Jenny was asking.

Noah put Sharon into the boat with Neil, then stood beside its bow keeping watch. No one else attempted to approach, and Noah was fairly sure there were no more of the slavers running loose on the island. He himself had killed several, and each of the others had claimed more than one life. In his initial reconnaissance, he had estimated that there were no more than two-dozen; since two of them were still alive, there probably weren't many others left, if any.

His headset came to life. "Noah?" Jenny said. "We are coming out."

"All right. Did you learn anything about Sarah?"

There was silence for a moment, and then he heard Jenny's sigh. "They said she was sold, all right," she said softly. "But, Noah—they said she put up a fight when her buyer tried to take her. Apparently they beat her pretty badly. The man who talked said—he said she didn't seem to be breathing when they loaded her into the helicopter."

Noah took a moment to digest what he had heard, then glanced around at Sharon Ingersoll. "We've got the mission objective," he said. "Let's get her to someplace we can clean her up and start coaching her on her new identity. I want to put her on a plane out of Pattaya sometime tomorrow. Once that's done, I'll start looking for Sarah."

"You mean *we'll* start looking for her," Jenny said. "I just completed a mission, they won't be sending me out for at least a couple of weeks. The boys and I will stick with you as long as we can." She seemed to hesitate for a second. "I tried to get the name of the buyer, but these guys didn't seem to know it. I had to settle for a couple of names they did know. Apparently, *Nay Thas* is run on an almost military-type structure. These guys said this camp was run by Captain Pak. According to them, we can find him and his lieutenant, a guy named Cho, right there in Pattaya. They run one of the Muay Thai arenas."

"Good," Noah said. "Then at least we know where to start."

Everyone but Noah and Marco climbed into the boat, and the two of them pushed it off the beach and back into the water before jumping in themselves. Noah clambered back to the tiller and threw the electric motor into reverse, backing it away from the beach before turning it around and shifting it into forward motion. This time, he didn't care how much noise the boat made and shoved the speed controller all the way to its stop.

Jenny settled herself next to Sharon, and put an arm around the girl. "Are you okay?"

Sharon, who had been barely able to hold herself together through the firefight, suddenly threw herself against Jenny as she dissolved into tears and hysterics. It took almost 15 minutes for her to get herself back under control, and then she slowly began to describe her ordeal.

"At first, there were just five of them," she said. "I tried to ignore it, to just let it happen, but they—they raped me, one after the other, and when they got done they let more of them come in. Over and over, it was like—it was horrible. Oh, God, I'm so ashamed!"

Jenny hugged her close and stroked her hair. "Shh," she said softly, "just let it go, let it out. It's okay to cry, honey, but you have to remember that you didn't do anything wrong. You were the one who got hurt, not the one who hurt someone else, and there's nothing for you to be ashamed of. And, as for those men? Every one of them is dead, now, and at least a couple of them got their dicks cut off or shot off before they died. None of them will ever do this to anyone else, and none of them will ever touch you again."

Sharon pulled back and looked up at her face, and then the tears began anew. Jenny hugged her tight once more, and gradually the girl's sobbing slowed and stopped.

When they got back to the boathouse, they cleaned up every trace of their presence on the boat and in the facility, then Jenny, Sharon and Neil got into the car with Dave and drove away. Noah and the others got onto the motorcycles and followed, as they traveled back into Pattaya and to their hotel.

Jenny took Sharon into her room, grabbing the girl's new carry-on bag with clean clothes and toiletries, while all of the men piled into Noah's. Jim, Randy and Dave simply made themselves as comfortable as they could on the floor, and they all were asleep within minutes.

Next door, Sharon spent most of an hour in the shower, until it ran so cold she had to get out. She put on some of the new clothes from the bag—Jenny had thrown her slavery clothes into the trash—and then the two of them lay together and held each other until shortly before dawn.

Noah let himself sleep until ten, but then his internal alarm clock woke him. The rest were still asleep, but it was time to start the next phase. He picked up his phone and dialed a number as the rest of them were forcing themselves awake.

"Thank you for calling Brigadoon Investments," came the same recorded voice, but Noah didn't wait for the rest of the message. He punched in the code that got him direct access to the off-hours operator, reported that he had located and retrieved the mission objective, and would be putting her on a plane later that day.

"Hold one," the operator said, and Noah listened to hold music for almost two minutes.

"Camelot? It's Allison. Tell me about Sarah."

"I have no concrete knowledge about Sarah," Noah said. "After interrogation of some of the men at the slave camp, we were told that she had been sold, but that she had put up a fight and did not appear to be breathing when she was taken away by helicopter. We have a couple of leads to check out, will do as soon as our mission objective is safely on her way out of the country."

Allison was silent for several seconds, and then Noah heard her curse softly. "Noah, don't assume she's dead. You find out exactly what happened, and if possible you bring her back alive. If not—if not, then I want you to kill every single one of the bastards responsible, you understand me?"

"Yes, Ma'am, I understand. Cinderella wants to stay and work with me on this for a while. Is that acceptable?"

"Hell, yes, it's acceptable! You're the best I've got, but Jenny's probably number two. Between the two of you and your teams, I expect you to do whatever it takes to find that girl and bring her home if she's alive."

"Yes, Ma'am," Noah said, and then the line went dead.

Jenny brought Sharon over to his room a few minutes later, and Randy and Neil were sent out for lunch. They came back twenty minutes later with buckets of honest-to-goodness KFC chicken and side dishes of rice and curry. The eight of them sat down to eat, as Noah began to explain to Sharon that her old life was completely over, and she was about to begin a new one.

"The problem," he explained, "is that Sharon Ingersoll now has an international criminal record and is listed worldwide as having escaped from prison in Thailand. The State Department doesn't want to take any chances on this coming back to haunt you, or them, at any time in the future. Since you are so valuable to DARPA, and since you have no living family, it was decided that the best thing to do was to create an entirely new identity for you. The people you work with have enough security clearances to be aware of the situation, so I'm going to provide you with your new identification, passport, luggage and everything today."

Sharon seemed surprised, but a part of her seemed to be relieved, as well. "So, Sharon is dead, then? Who am I now, can you tell me that?"

Noah nodded. "Yes," he said, and he handed her the purse that had been intended for her. "Your new name is Alexis Stratton, and you're from Bakersfield, California. There's a letter in the purse that will tell you more about your new life history, and when you get home, you'll be going through some intense training to make it come naturally to you. For now, you only need to memorize your name, date of birth and your new passport number. As soon as you're ready, we can take you to the airport and put you on a plane back to the states."

It took about two more hours for Sharon to accept the situation, but she finally looked at Jenny and smiled. "All that happened last night," she said, "that was when Sharon died. None of that ever happened to me. Not to Alexis, y'know?"

Noah cocked his head to one side and looked at her. "If you can hold onto that thought," he said, "if you can cling to that and wrap your pain around it, then you're already on the way to recovery. You're still going to have some rough times, I'm sure, but if you can hang on tight to that way of thinking, then I believe you will get through it."

At just after three that afternoon, Jenny, Neil and Marco took Alexis to the airport and put her on a flight that would take her back to Arlington, Virginia, where a new home awaited her. She thanked each of them before they left, and even kissed Neil and Marco and Jenny just before she boarded the plane that would take her to Switzerland for her first layover.

When Jenny and the two men returned, Noah finally told them about his phone conversation with Allison, and

Jenny smiled. "Good thing she said it was okay," she said, "cause I wasn't leaving you. Let's go find this Captain Pak and make him talk, shall we?"

TWENTY-FIVE

Neil looked at her, then glanced at Noah. "I, uh, I did a little research last night, while the rest of you were sleeping," he said. "I found Pak, and he apparently owns the Pattaya Muay Thai Champions' Arena, down off Walking Street."

"Walking Street?" Noah asked.

"Yeah, that's what it's called. It's sort of a long shopping and nightclub area, and it's been blocked off to keep cars out. Champions' Arena is really just a training gym on one of the alleys that lead off it. I guess there have been some pretty good fighters who have trained there." He paused and looked meaningfully at Noah. "It's also a place where some of the deadliest fighters in the world hang out, so I'd suggest we all go, and go armed, if you plan to ask this guy any questions he might object to."

"What time does it close?" Noah asked.

Neil's eyebrows went up a notch. "I don't think it does," he said. "From what I read, this Pak is there most of the time. I'm guessing we know where he is when he's gone."

Noah nodded. "Then let's go," he said. Each of the men tucked a Glock into the back of his pants and put a light jacket over it. Neil hung his Uzi from his shoulder by its strap, and it hung nicely and concealed when he put his own jacket on.

Jenny slung her purse over her shoulder and led the way out the door. Once again, she, Dave and Neil rode in the car, while the rest climbed onto the motorcycles and followed. Neil had called the gym up on his GPS, and it led them to a parking area close to Walking Street.

From there, they went on foot. The area was extremely crowded, and they saw a number of Western tourists. Jenny pointed out that all of the dozens of bars they saw had sexily dressed girls standing in front of them, flirting with every male that walked by. Neil actually blushed more than once, when girls would run up to him and try to press themselves against his long legs.

They reached the alley after only a few minutes, and had no trouble locating Champions' Arena. The place was brightly lighted, with neon signs proclaimed it as the home gymnasium of several Muay Thai past champions. They stopped and looked it over for a moment before they entered, and then Jenny led the way once again.

"Mr. Pak?" Jenny said to the first man she saw. "I'm looking for Mr. Pak, is he around?"

That man called to another one, who hurried over and looked at Jenny. "I am so sorry," he said, "but my friend, he does not speak English. What can I do to help you?"

"Oh, thank you," Jenny said. "I'm looking for Mr. Pak, can you tell me where to find him?"

The man looked at her somewhat suspiciously. "Mr. Pak? May I ask why you wish to see him?"

Jenny smiled sweetly and pointed at Noah. "Because I think my fighter, here, can beat his fighters. I thought maybe we could set up a match, and both of us make some money."

The man's eyebrows rose as he looked at Noah over, but

he nodded once and asked Jenny to wait. He turned and jogged across the room, and Jenny turned to look at Noah.

"Hey, I know a little bit about Muay Thai," she said. "It's called the art of eight limbs, because you use essentially every part of your body in fighting. Knees, elbows, they're just as important as feet and fists, and if you don't know what you're doing, the other guy's elbow can be downright deadly."

Neil leaned around Noah and glared at her. "And you just challenged this guy to let Noah fight one of his people? Holy crap, you really are insane, aren't you?"

"No, she's not," Noah said. He was closely watching two men in a boxing ring who were sparring, and his eyes were following every move they made. "I see what they're doing, and it's simply logical. In order to get the maximum effect from your limbs in a fight, you need to minimize the amount of motion necessary to deliver the force you want to apply. It isn't necessary to swing your whole arm to punch with a fist if you can deliver the same amount of force with an elbow or knee."

Neil looked at the boxing ring, then back to Noah. He started to speak, but Marco interrupted him.

"Boss, I got to agree with the kid. You get in a ring with one of those guys, we'll be scraping you up with a spoon."

"Well, don't worry about it," Jenny said. "I sincerely doubt our friend Pak is going to accept the challenge from some *farang* bitch who walks in off the street, no matter how big her fighter seems to be. All I'm really trying to do is get his attention, and if he's like a lot of Thais I've known, failing to come out and speak with me would be similar to a Japanese losing face. Hush, here comes the messenger."

The man they had spoken to ran back up to Jenny and

bowed respectfully, then looked her in the eye. "Mr. Pak, he says please come to his office." He turned and started walking away, expecting them to follow.

They did so, and a moment later they were ushered into a large and luxurious office room. Pak was sitting behind the desk, and the expression on his face indicated that he was not feeling amused.

"Which of these children is your fighter?" Pak asked.

Jenny pointed at Noah. "This is him," she said. "I'm new in the area, but I know a champion when I see one, and this is the next one. Do you have anyone who can fight in his class? I'm curious to see how long one of yours can stay in the ring with mine."

A smile began slowly to spread across Pak's face, and then he began to laugh. "You are all Americans," he said, "*farangs*. This is the first time any group of Americans has entered my arena, and the timing of your arrival leads me to think that scheduling a match is not what you genuinely have in mind."

Jenny smiled and looked inquisitive. "Oh, really? And what do you think my real reason might be for coming to see you?"

"I believe it may have something to do with certain unfortunate events that took place late last night," Pak replied, "on a certain island not far from here. Am I correct? Please respect me enough to be honest. And do not expect me to be frightened, even though I see that you and your men are armed. There are more than two-dozen of my trainees in the building, and I have already told my assistants to alert them. If you attempt to harm me in any way, none of you will make it out of this place alive."

Jenny laughed delightedly, and leaned forward to put her hands on the edge of Pak's desk. "You are indeed correct," she said. "I'm afraid we paid a visit to your friends on that island last night in search of a friend of our own. Unfortunately, we did not find her, but one of your men was extremely happy to tell us that you should be able to provide us with information about where she's gone."

Pak leaned back and folded his hands over his stomach. "Why would you believe that I would know anything about your friend?"

"Oh, did I leave that part out? You see, your man was good enough to tell me that he saw you sell our friend to someone else. Now, where we come from, people don't get bought and sold, so that kind of bothers us. We can settle this whole thing in a hurry though, if you'll just tell us who bought her, and where she was taken."

Pak cocked his head to one side and looked at her, then looked at the men with her. "Ah," he said, "you must refer to the little blonde flower. I am so sorry, but it is with great regret that I must tell you that your friend is no longer among the living."

Neil surged forward suddenly, and the little Uzi appeared in his hand as if by magic. "You're a liar," he screamed. "Now tell us where she is, or I'll blow your ass away!"

Pak grinned at him. "You may kill me if you wish," he said, "but it will not change the fact that the little flower has indeed withered. It will also only bring on your own death, for my men are standing outside this room, prepared to kill each and every one of you unless I call them off." He continued to stare into Neil's eyes, and the young man's resolve began to waver. After a moment, he lowered the gun and stepped back behind Noah once again.

Noah's expression had not changed, and no one standing nearby would have thought Pak's words had any effect on him, but something inside Noah snapped with a crack as loud as thunder. For a split second, he wondered where he had heard—felt—that sound before, and then he realized that it was on the day, when he was only a child, that his father had killed his mother and then himself. Whatever emotion had been trying to come back to life in Noah Wolf was suddenly dragged to a precipice, and was teetering on the edge.

Jenny looked at Neil and smiled, then turned back to Pak. "Let's just say I find it hard to believe you," she said. "If you say she's dead, tell me how she died."

"She tried to attack one of my men, and he took exception to it. Unfortunately, he does not know his own strength. The kick he gave to her head, I am afraid, proved to be fatal."

Neil suddenly began to cry, tears streaming down his face. Noah glanced at him, but then turned back to face Pak. "Where's her body?" he asked.

Pak spread his hands. "When one of these girls dies, she is cremated. Her ashes are then placed in a beautiful garden, so that her spirit may enjoy beauty until it is time for her to be reborn."

Noah stood there for a moment, then cocked his head slightly to one side. "If she died yesterday, would she be cremated already?"

"But of course she would," Pak said. "She would have no family to mourn her, no friends to attend a funeral; there is no point in delay. She was taken to the monks for cremation early this morning, and they were grateful for the gifts we gave them in return for the service."

Jenny looked at Noah and raised an eyebrow, but he didn't give her any response. She turned back to Pak. "We are prepared to kill you, and then try to fight our way out of here," she said, "but personally, I prefer to do things the easy way. If you would take us to her ashes, we could be on our way, and you would not need to see us again."

Pak looked her in the eye. "Is this a genuine offer?" he asked. "I would be willing to avoid the bloodshed, if it is."

Jenny nodded. "It's genuine," she said. "Take us to proof that she is dead, and we will be on our way."

Pak slowly rose from his chair, and nodded his head. "Follow me," he said, and walked out the door into the gym. A dozen of his trainees stepped back, each of them obviously prepared to fight, but Pak waved a hand and they all walked away.

They followed him out a back door of the building, and several of the trainees followed them as they walked down the long alley to a small temple surrounded by trees and bushes. A monk was sitting outside the temple, and looked up at Pak with a smile.

Pak spoke in Thai, and the monk instantly rose and went inside. A moment later, he returned with another monk who looked at Pak and said, "Yes, old friend?"

"These people were friends of the little flower who passed from the earth," Pak said. "Can you show them to her ashes?"

"Indeed," the monk said, bowing to him. He looked at the Americans and smiled. "If you would come this way, please."

They followed him around the temple to a small garden, where a number of monks were sitting in poses of meditation and prayer. They were led past them all, to a small flower garden, and the monk turned to them. "We spread her ashes here," he said softly, "and to commemorate her life, we have taken some of her hair and strewn it among the petals."

He pointed down, and Noah saw a lock of blonde hair lying among the flowers. It appeared to be fresh and new, and he saw that it was exactly the color of Sarah's hair.

He stared at it for a moment, and then turned and started walking back the way they had come. Jenny and the others watched him for a moment, and then hurried to catch up to him.

They returned to the hotel without any of them speaking, and Noah began packing. He called Darryl Knapp and told him to come and pick up the equipment, then told Neil and Marco to get ready to return home.

Neil grabbed his arm. "Noah, we can't…"

"The hair I saw was Sarah's," Noah said. "The way it was curled is from her twirling it whenever she gets frustrated with me."

"But, but maybe they only clipped it off her and planted it there," Neil sputtered, but Noah put a hand on his shoulder and stopped him.

"Neil, I can't imagine they'd go to such an elaborate length as that. How would they know we'd come asking about her? Why would they bother setting this up at all?"

"But…"

"Let's go home, Neil," Noah said. "We won't forget her, but there's nothing more we can do here."

Neil walked away, and Jenny came to Noah. "I don't get it," she said. "You walked away and left Pak alive. If you honestly believe that Sarah is dead, why would you do that?"

Noah looked at her for a long moment, then shrugged his shoulders. "More violence isn't going to bring her back," he said. "I'll just save it for the next mission."

She leaned her head to the left and stared at him for

a few more seconds, then shook her head and walked away. Noah watched her go, before looking around at all the members of the two teams that were gathered in the room.

Which one of you is the traitor? Noah asked himself silently.

Read on for a sneak peak of Black Sheep (Noah Wolf book 6), or buy your copy now:
davidarcherbooks.com/black-sheep

Be the first to receive Noah Wolf updates. Sign up here:
davidarcherbooks.com/noah-updates

DAVID ARCHER

BLACK SHEEP

A
NOAH WOLF
THRILLER

RIGHT HOUSE

PROLOGUE

Noah Wolf packed his things while Neil and Marco prepared their own. The three of them spoke only when it was absolutely necessary, and usually in sentences of fewer than five words. Sarah's loss was weighing heavily on them all, and none of them, not even Marco, wanted to make it seem more real by talking about it.

There was a knock on the door and Neil turned to open it. Jenny was standing there, her own team behind her with their luggage.

"You guys about ready?" she asked. "I don't think I can stand this place much longer."

"Another minute," Noah said. "Our flight doesn't leave for a few hours, there's not exactly a rush to get to the airport. I was thinking about grabbing some lunch on the way."

Neil scoffed. "Geez," he said, "are you serious? Damn, Noah, even I can't think about food right now. Sarah's gone," he choked out, "doesn't that affect you at all?"

Noah looked at him, but his expression remained stoic. "There's a hole in my world," he said. He turned back to Jenny. "We'll be ready in five minutes. You guys can go on with the rental car, we'll meet you at the airport and get some lunch at one of the restaurants there."

Jenny nodded and turned away without a word. The other three men followed her as Neil closed the door again. He stood there with his back to Noah for a moment, then released the doorknob and turned around.

"Look, Noah," he said haltingly, "I'm sorry about that. Maybe you don't feel things the way we do, but I know how important Sarah was to you. I shouldn't have said that, and I really do apologize."

"Let it go," Noah said. "We each have to deal with the reality in front of us. That's how life works, remember?"

They finished packing and went down to check out of the hotel, then Marco chose a taxi at random. The car was small, and the driver used a bungee cord to hold the trunk closed over their luggage as they got into it. A moment later, they were on the way to the airport.

Noah was in the front seat with Marco behind him, and Neil was behind the driver. He watched Noah as the car rolled along, noticing how the big man watched the city passing by. There was something in Noah's demeanor that Neil felt was different, but he couldn't put his finger on it.

* * *

Mr. Pak watched the Americans walk away, then turned to the monk.

"Did they believe you?" he asked.

The monk met his gaze. "The cold one recognized the locks of hair. Strewn among the ashes, they imply that we honored her according to our customs."

Pak nodded solemnly. "Agreed. I suspect that if you were doubted, both of us would soon be prepared for our own burials. The cold one, as you called him, is an American assassin, as is the woman. The lives of monks and businessmen would mean little to them."

He turned and left the temple, returning to the gym. There was no sign that the Americans had stopped there, so he went back into his office and relaxed. Lom, his most trusted man, stepped inside and bowed respectfully to him.

"They are gone," Pak said. "Prepare the girl for her journey. I want her out of the country before midnight."

Lom bowed once again and walked out of the room. Now in his fifties and showing the thinning that comes to an aging athlete, he had once been among the most respected of *Muay Thai* trainers. He passed through the parting sea of fighters and students that crowded the gym as he made his way to a door at the rear, then opened it and stepped through, descending the stairs into the basement. One of the many students who revered him, one of the many who hoped to earn a place in *Nay Thas* by his side, sat on a chair beside yet another door and rose as Lom approached. Without a word, he opened the door and let his Master step through it.

The girl lay on the mat that had been placed on the floor, curled up on her side. Her head turned as Lom entered the room, but she only groaned when she saw that it was him again. He had been the one who had seemed to buy her on the island, and it had been he who had taken charge of her on the boat, lifted her from it and carried her like a lifeless doll to whatever excuse for a doctor they used. The wizened physician had pronounced her alive, if somewhat bruised and with a mild concussion. She would live and could travel, and that was all that seemed to matter to these people.

"Can you stand?" Lom asked in perfect English.

"Screw you," the girl said. A hand went to her head and stroked what remained of her hair. It was less than an inch long, and the filth of the mat had turned it from blonde to a dirty gray.

"I do not wish to hurt you," Lom said. "If you will get up, I can see that you are fed and able to wash. You will be taking a journey this evening, and it is up to me to see that you are as comfortable as possible. I even have clean clothing for you."

She rolled onto her back and simply looked up at him for several seconds, then extended a hand. Lom stared warily into her eyes for a moment, then carefully reached out and took it in his own to help her to her feet.

She was not quite standing when she suddenly yanked him forward and threw a kick at his head, but he blocked it easily with an elbow, then caught her ankle in his hand. He had expected it, of course; she was a captured American agent and would be seeking any opportunity to gain the upper hand, even for a moment. Thrown off balance, she fell back onto the mat on her backside and his foot stopped barely short of crushing her throat.

"Men and women who have trained for years in *Muay Thai* are unable to successfully attack me," he said calmly. "Whatever training you have received, it will not be sufficient to allow you to overcome me. Please do not attempt it again, for I was speaking truth when I said I do not wish to hurt you."

She glared up at him, but when he pulled on her hand again she got to her feet. When he stepped aside and pointed toward the door, she shuffled slowly through it, favoring her right hip. The rip in the pants she was wearing allowed Lom to see the bruise that had spread on it, and he resolved to punish the fool who had damaged the girl. The entire party had been warned that she was of great value; there was no excuse for the condition she had been in when they had brought her to him. The old physician had said she suffered no permanent or serious injury, but valuable property must be handled with care. That fool would be an example to the rest, so that such problems could be avoided in the future.

He followed her out of the room and pointed to another door across the basement. "There is a bathroom in there, and I have already left some clothing in it for you. There is soap for your body and your hair, so that you may at least feel clean. Go and wash, and I will have food brought to you."

"I'm not hungry," she said. She limped toward the door and opened it, then stepped inside and pulled it closed behind her.

The man who had been guarding her raised an eyebrow at Lom, but said nothing. "Leave her alone," Lom said. "She is not to be disturbed as she bathes." He walked over to the bathroom door and slid a bolt into place, locking her in, before he turned and went back up the stairs.

Inside the bathroom, the girl heard the bolt slide home and then slowly began stripping off the filthy clothing she had worn since being taken from the prison. They stank, both from her sweat and the fact that she had been locked in a box with her own urine. She sat down naked on the toilet and made use of it, resenting the gratitude she felt for being allowed such a small touch of dignity.

When she was finished, she stood and stepped into the bathtub beside it. There was a curtain on a rod, and she pulled it across out of habit as she turned on the water and set it to be as hot as she could stand before pulling up the lever that would redirect it to the shower head. It came out cold at first, and she gasped, but then the hot water made it up the pipe and she let it flow over her head and down her body. The heat felt good.

After a moment, she pulled her head out from under the shower and looked around. There was a bar of soap and a small bottle on a shelf, and it wasn't long before she had scrubbed herself red. Once her body was clean, she used a handful of shampoo on the short remnants of her once-flowing blonde locks.

By the time she had rinsed herself off, the water was starting to cool. She turned it off and pulled back the curtain, found the towel that was hanging beside the tub, and rubbed herself dry. She tossed the towel onto the floor and stepped out onto it, then picked up the pair of jeans from the back of the toilet and slid into them before pulling the t-shirt over her head. They fit fairly well and were comfortable, despite the fact that she had no bra or panties.

She heard the bolt slide back, and then Lom opened the door just a crack. "Are you dressed?"

"Would it matter?" she asked. "Since when do animals like you have any respect for a woman's modesty?"

There was no answer. A second later, the door opened the rest of the way and she saw that he was holding a tray. There was a bowl on the tray, along with a bottle of some kind of juice.

"I brought the food anyway," he said. "As I told you, you will be going on a journey. I don't know how soon you will be able to eat again, so I suggest you take advantage of the opportunity now."

She glared at him, but then reached out and picked up the bowl. It was full of rice, with fish and pork and some sort of sauce mixed into it, and when she lifted a spoonful to her mouth she realized that she truly was hungry. Perhaps that was the reason it tasted so good. She'd read somewhere that hunger was the best sauce of all; it might have been true.

Lom turned and pointed, and she saw that he had set up a small table with a chair, so she carried the bowl over and sat down. She took another bite as he set the tray on the table, then looked up at him.

"So, where am I going?" she asked. "Somewhere close by? Some rich man's playground?"

"I'm afraid I cannot give that answer to you," Lom said. "I can only tell you that you will be leaving Thailand by boat. Someone has paid a very high price for you."

"For me? Then somebody is going to be disappointed. I'd rather die than become somebody's little sex toy, and not everyone has had the kind of training you have."

Lom's eyes narrowed as he looked at her. "Sex toy? I'm afraid you might soon prefer that fate to whatever awaits you. There may be many reasons behind your buyer's insistence on purchasing you, but I am quite certain that not one of them has anything to do with sex."

The girl looked at him askance. "Why not? Isn't that what you bastards do? Round up girls and sell them as sex slaves?"

"That is indeed a profitable business, but you have proven to be far more valuable than that. Are you truly surprised to find that there are those who will pay well for a captured American agent?"

She managed to keep the surprise out of her face, but her eyes gave it away. Despite her denials, she knew exactly what he was saying. "American agent? I'm just a girl who got busted for trying to buy some drugs."

Lom smiled at her. "Ms. Child, please do not think me stupid. We know exactly who you are, and who you work for."

She looked him in the eye for another second, then lowered her gaze to the bowl in front of her as she took another bite. "Boy, have you got the wrong girl. My name is Kayla Maguire, and I work for Dempsey's Department Store back in Omaha."

The smile didn't waver. "No. Your name is Sarah Child, and you are an agent of the United States organization known as E & E. Your duties normally include being the driver for the American assassin whose code name is Camelot. We know this because the information was provided to us by a CIA informant who was involved in preparing the plan for your insertion into the prison, and it was quite costly."

Her eyes rose slowly back to his face, and he could see the defeat in them. She stared at him for almost a minute, then put another bite into her mouth. She picked up the bottle of juice and took a long drink from it, never letting her eyes move from his own.

"CIA sold me out?" she asked. "Who was it? Can you tell me?"

"I do not have that information. However, does it truly matter? The fact is that you have been compromised. As I understand it, your government will never acknowledge your existence. Should they ever admit that you and your compatriots were in Thailand to perpetrate an escape from our prison system, it would create an international incident, and could well be considered an act of war. Once you are captured, you become useless to them. Your only value now is in the information that can be extracted from you."

"Then you're still screwed," Sarah said. "As you pointed out, I'm just a driver. I don't exactly get briefed on any important state secrets."

"I'm certain you do not, but you know, at the very least, what your mission objective was, and I'm certain you know a great deal about the organization you work for and how it functions. I would naturally suppose that this is the information your buyer hopes to obtain. Considering how valuable such information seems to be, there is little doubt that those who bought you will stop at nothing to get it."

The fear in her eyes shone through for a moment before she could hide it, but then she put on a brave face. "I don't know that much," she said. "They can do their worst, but they're not going to get anything worth having."

Lom shrugged his shoulders. "That does not matter to me, of course. My duties only involve getting you ready for the journey. If you have finished eating, then I should be taking you to the docks."

"Keep your panties on," Sarah said, and she picked up the spoon again. "Like you said, I don't know when I'll get the chance to eat again." She shoved another bite into her mouth, then cocked her head to the left. "And just so you know, while my government might do nothing to try to get me back, that doesn't mean I won't be rescued. Remember that assassin, the one known as Camelot? His number one rule is that he never leaves anyone behind. I feel sorry for you when he finds out I was here."

"I don't think I have anything to worry about," Lom said. "You see, he was here just an hour ago, and he was taken to the temple and shown evidence that you are dead. Our contact says he is already making preparations to return to the United States."

Sarah stopped chewing. "No," she said, "that's not possible."

ONE

The flight from Pattaya back to Denver took nearly a day and a half, with a total of four layovers along the way. It was already after ten PM when Noah and the rest were finally able to leave the airport and head back to Kirtland.

Jenny and her team had come back with them, but they had a van of their own waiting in long-term parking. By pure coincidence, it was parked only three spaces away from Neil's big Hummer, so they drove out of the parking lot and hit the highway together. Dave Lange drove the van, and kept it on Neil's tail until the Hummer peeled off the exit and onto the highway that would take it to Noah's house.

"What do you think will happen now?" Neil asked as he drove along the dark road. "Will there be a funeral, a memorial service?"

"Of course," Marco said. "Neverland never forgets her people. Sarah was one of its best, so you can be sure Allison is planning something big for her."

"Won't matter," Neil said, and there was a sniffle in it. "Sarah's gone, and it just won't be right to have someone else in her place. Especially not right after we lost Moose, y'know? She shouldn't have even been in that prison, they should've sent Jenny or someone like that in there. Not Sarah. She was just too—she was too nice, y'know what I mean?"

"Let it go, Neil," Noah said. "There's nothing you can do, and it wasn't your fault. You have to let it go or it'll eat you alive."

"Yeah, and that's from the man who can't even grieve over the woman who loved him. Forgive me, boss, if I don't think you're all that qualified to advise me on emotional matters, okay?"

"We all grieve in our own ways, Neil," Marco said, but Neil cut him off.

"Not him," he said. "Noah doesn't grieve at all. He doesn't even know how."

The kid shook himself, then, as if he was just hearing the things that were coming out of his own mouth. "Noah," he said, "man, I'm sorry, I didn't mean any of that..."

"Let it go, Neil," Noah said.

Noah and Jenny had both called in before leaving Thailand, and both were scheduled for debriefing the following morning, Noah at nine AM and Jenny at eleven. Noah climbed out of the Hummer and walked into his house without even saying goodbye to Neil and Marco. Marco got into his own car and drove away while Neil cut across the yard to park beside the trailer he rented from Noah.

Inside the house, Noah dropped his luggage and went into the bathroom. He took a quick shower, then walked into the bedroom and pulled the covers down on the bed and climbed into it. He set an alarm on his phone and closed his eyes, drifting to sleep only a few minutes later.

Noah Wolf dreamed only rarely, and most of his

dreams involved the afternoon his parents had died. That was the tragic event that had shaped the rest of his life by leaving him completely devoid of emotion. It was a rare form of PTSD known as histrionic affect disorder, but rather than cripple him, the condition had allowed him to form a code of ethics all his own, one that made him the incredibly efficient soldier and killer he had become.

On this particular night, however, he had a dream that was completely unrelated to that tragedy.

He was lying in bed, and suddenly felt Sarah's arms go around him. He turned his head to look at her and saw her face. It was bruised and bloodied, and the expression it wore was a pleading one.

"I'm not dead, Noah," she said in a hoarse whisper. "Don't leave me behind."

"I won't," he replied. "But I have to find the trail before I can come for you. I won't give up, I promise you. Stay strong, Sarah, and I'll find you."

She stared at him through bloodshot eyes for a moment, then shook her head. "No, you won't," she said, and then she was gone.

Noah awoke instantly and turned to look at her side of the bed. For the first time in many years, it took him almost an hour to get back to sleep.

When the alarm went off, Noah rose and dressed quickly, then made himself a cup of instant coffee and carried it to the Corvette. He started the car up and backed out of the drive, then hit the road toward Allison's office in the conference room.

He arrived ten minutes early, but Allison's secretary told him to go on in. Donald Jefferson was already there, just setting out the doughnuts, and Allison came in only a moment later.

"Report, Camelot," she said. "Tell me what the hell went wrong out there."

Noah had not shared his suspicions with anyone yet, and especially not over cell phones that were on two separate continents. When he had called in, he'd simply said that he would make a full report during his debriefing.

"Somebody sold Sarah out," he said. "I haven't figured out who yet, but I suspect it was someone on my team. While I don't believe Neil would ever betray her, I haven't ruled him out as a suspect. If it was one of mine, I'd have to put my suspicions on Marco."

Allison didn't seem surprised, but Donald Jefferson leaned forward. "Sold out to whom?"

"I have no information about that," Noah said. "While it may have been coincidental that Sarah was taken from the prison, the fact that she was in the possession of the *Nay Thas* and was then sold to someone before she was broken and trained tells me that the buyer had to have known something about who she really is. When I saw what was obviously lots of her hair scattered among ashes at the temple, I realized that she had not only been compromised, but was being turned over to someone for interrogation."

"And yet you did nothing about it before leaving Thailand," Allison said. "That sounds odd, Noah, especially for you."

"Pak involved the monks of the temple in the deception, so that tells me this is a lot bigger than just trying to cover up a girl sold into sexual slavery. While I might have gotten some information on where she was taken by torturing him, the people he surrounds himself with make it more likely that we all would have died in the attempt. I had to decide whether it was more important to attempt to retrieve her or to find out how she was compromised and identify the traitor, and I chose the latter. The security of E & E has to take precedence over the life of any particular agent. Once I know how this happened, I'm going to request permission to go back after her."

"Then you believe whoever has her was told who she is and who she works for?" Allison asked.

Noah nodded. "Logically, it's the only scenario that makes sense. I've gone over the mission repeatedly, and every member of both teams had at least one opportunity to make contact with someone, and that includes our people in Thailand."

Allison nodded back. "I agree with your conclusions," she said. "I've already got CIA working on our people over there, to see if any of them might have been compromised, but the reports thus far are clean. As for your team and Jenny's, I frankly find it hard to believe that any of them could have betrayed us this way, but I can't deny that I've seen it happen before. Agents who seem loyal and trustworthy may harbor feelings of resentment or dissatisfaction that lead them to betray teammates, organizations, even the country. At this point, no one is above suspicion." She looked him calmly in the eye. "That includes you, Noah."

Noah nodded. "Of course. I've been considering possible avenues of investigation, but I wanted to discuss all of this with you before making any recommendations."

Allison shook her head. "First, you made the statement a moment ago that every member of both teams had at least one chance to make contact and sell Sarah out. Explain."

"There are three logical possibilities." He held up one finger. "First, the people who took Sarah out of the prison may have known already who she was, and the roundup of girls may have been nothing but a smokescreen to hide the fact that they were after her in particular. If that were the case, then the most logical scenario would indicate someone from the E & E station in Bangkok, or it could be that either Marco or Neil made contact with a foreign agent and revealed that she was coming in. Marco was out of my sight twice before she got to the prison, and Neil is capable of making contact with anyone through his computers, possibly even right under my nose."

Noah held up a second finger. "The second possibility is that the roundup actually was coincidental, and that the unknown persons who took her were contacted after the fact. Marco and Neil are still possible suspects, but now we have added factors: Jenny and her team. Jenny spent several hours inside the prison posing as Sarah's sister, and it's possible she was compromised and gave up information to save herself, or sold it to benefit financially. David Lange went out with Neil to purchase some equipment, and could have made contact while he was out of Neil's sight. Randy Mitchell and Jim Marino also had opportunities to communicate with someone unobserved."

"Have any of them displayed what you would consider atypical behavior?" Jefferson asked.

"Nothing that I can specifically identify. Neil has acted perfectly normal for Neil, and while it's possible he could have done this, I personally find it inconceivable. Marco seems occasionally dissatisfied with my decisions, but he never offered me any argument and always obeyed my orders. Jenny's team is unfamiliar to me, but their behaviors were consistent from the moment I met them."

"What about the third possibility?" Allison asked.

"At Jenny's suggestion, we involved two women from

the E & E station in Pattaya. It's entirely possible that one or both of them have some sort of contact with Pak and the *Nay Thas*. If so, the fact that an E & E agent had been captured in the roundup might have been too tempting an opportunity to pass up. That information would undoubtedly be extremely valuable."

Allison leaned back in her chair and looked at him. "I detest the thought that any of my people could have done something like this," she said, "but I can't find any flaws in your deductions. As I mentioned previously, I have CIA going over all of the communication and activity logs of our people over there, and they haven't found anything yet that could be a discrepancy. What do you recommend as the next step?"

"I considered suggesting polygraph tests, but most of the people in our line of work could probably beat one. What about a deception expert? From everything I've read, it's impossible to prevent the minute facial expressions and body language they watch for."

Allison frowned and ran a hand over her face. "It's difficult, but not impossible, and especially not for anyone with psychopathic or sociopathic tendencies. Unfortunately, the people best suited for this work display some of those. Donald and I have both been trained in deception detection, but we've been fooled in the past." She turned to Jefferson. "Donald? Any suggestions?"

Jefferson chewed his cheek for a couple of seconds, then nodded his head. "The thing to do is keep whoever betrayed us unbalanced. We've got the situation in Pyongyang that we need to deal with right away; it's complicated and dangerous, so my thought is to tell Jenny that Cinderella and Camelot work so well together that we've decided a joint operation between them is what we need for that mission. Put them back together and in the field again, with no time to rest, and give Noah a better chance to observe them."

"Then you're convinced Noah is not the one who sold Sarah out?"

"I don't think he could possibly have done it unless it somehow benefited the mission, and it certainly did not. As of this moment, Noah is the only one in this group that I trust completely."

"Good," Allison said. "We are agreed on that." She turned to Noah. "Noah, there are four CIA agents in North Korea who have been captured, and unfortunately they possess a great deal of knowledge regarding certain Top Secret plans that the president has authorized in dealing with the little madman who runs the country there. CIA says rescue is impossible, so they have requested immediate termination of all four in order to maintain National Security. We were about to brief Hercules on the mission today, but I'm going to accept Donald's recommendation. Because the mission will be difficult and dangerous, we're going to send you and Jenny and your people on this one."

"Yes, Ma'am," Noah said. "May I ask a question?"

"Go ahead."

"Sarah has been captured, and she also possesses secret information. Will she be sanctioned?"

Allison leaned forward and looked him in the eye. "How long do you think she can hold out under interrogation?"

"Sarah is tougher than she thinks she is," Noah said. "She's loyal to the organization, but she'll regard any demand to give up information about our organization as being forced to betray me as well as E & E. Combined, both of those factors will keep her from any betrayal until she's subjected to enough pain to make her willing to die to escape it. Once that happens, the thought of dying will mean she won't have to face any of us if she betrays us, so she can give up something in the hope of getting what she wants, which at that point will be death. Depending on the level of torture, we could be talking anywhere from three days to a week."

Allison paused for a second then went on. "The most damaging information she could give up would involve the secret areas around Kirtland, and perhaps a few of our proprietary procedures or some of the inventions Wally's kids come up with. The world intelligence community already suspects that we exist, and neither my name nor Donald's is any secret in those circles. She might compromise your team, but we could simply switch up identities again and put you right back in the field." She leaned back and put her elbows on the arms of the chair, steepling her fingers in front of her face. "Noah, I won't authorize a sanction on Sarah. I don't think she knows enough to do us any real harm, and frankly, I want her back. That means you've got no more than a week to identify the traitor *and* find out where Sarah has been taken. I'm going to authorize unlimited resources for you on these two missions."

She sat forward again. "Go home. Tell Neil and Marco that you're being briefed on an urgent new mission at one o'clock this afternoon, and will be flying out tonight. I'll explain that to Jenny during her debrief this morning, so you'll all be here at one."

"Yes, Ma'am," Noah said, as he rose and started toward the door.

"Noah?" Allison said.

He stopped and turned to face her. "Yes?"

"When you identify the traitor," she said, "your orders are to terminate with extreme prejudice."

Noah nodded once. "Yes, Ma'am," he said. He walked out the door and was on the way home a few minutes later. As he drove, he took his phone out of his pocket and called Neil.

"Mmpf," the boy said, trying to rouse himself from sleep. "Wassup?"

"Emergency mission," Noah said. "Get yourself awake and head over to the house. We've got an emergency briefing at one, and we're going to be flying out tonight."

"What?" Neil sputtered, and Noah heard Lacey's voice in the background asking what was wrong. "We just got in!"

"As I said, it's an emergency mission. I'll call Marco now, so he'll know to make the briefing. And just so you know, Team Cinderella is going with us on this one. The Dragon Lady likes the way we work together."

"Oh, God," Neil mumbled. "Jenny scares the crap out of me. That woman is just plain evil." He let out a long sigh. "Okay, boss, whatever you say. I'm getting up."

Noah ended the call and punched the icon for Marco. Unlike Neil, Marco was already awake.

"Hey, boss," he said. "To what do I owe the pleasure?"

"We've got an emergency mission," Noah said. "Briefing at one o'clock."

"Geez, already? Doesn't that break some kind of rule, sending us out again this quick?"

"The Dragon Lady thinks it's necessary, and she makes the rules. See you at the briefing."

"You got it," Marco said, and then the line went dead.

Noah drove on to his house, deep in thought. No matter

how many times he went over what he remembered of the snafu'd mission, he couldn't make the facts line up enough to identify a particular traitor. Until he had some idea of who had sold Sarah out, it was going to be hard to find any leads on where she'd been taken, unless he retraced his steps and went back to Pattaya.

The problem was that trying to find out anything from Pak would still be likely to result in a bloodbath, and Noah couldn't go after Sarah if he was dead.

* * *

Sarah was driven to the dock in the back of a van with no windows, but it wouldn't have mattered if she had been able to see out. She didn't know anything about the area, and had no way to signal anyone. If Lom had been correct, there was no one to signal in any case.

At first, when Lom had told her that Noah was leaving her behind, she had refused to believe it. Later, however, it dawned on her that if he truly believed she was dead, his logical mind would see no reason to remain. He would go home, and go on with his life without her.

That was the hardest part for her, the knowledge that he wouldn't even grieve for her loss. It wasn't his fault, she knew that, but still...

When they arrived at the dock, she was quickly taken out of the van and hustled onto a large motor yacht. The boat was big enough for her to think of it more as a ship, but she only saw its stern. She was hustled down a flight of stairs and pushed into a room. She heard the door lock as soon as it was closed.

She seemed to be in a stateroom, a nice one with its own en-suite head. She had only showered a short time earlier, and she remembered what Noah had always told her about resting whenever she could, so she lay down on the bed and tried to relax.

Her mind was racing, though. Just the thought of someone betraying her, someone she had worked with and trusted, was more than she could take, but if it was anyone close to her, she was convinced it had to have been Marco. Noah would never do such a thing, and it was impossible to even entertain the thought that Neil might.

Of course, there were other possibilities. The local station chief was going to be aware of their mission, and who knew how many others? That thought made her feel a little better, at least; perhaps it wasn't someone she knew, but a perfect stranger who had done this to her.

The huge diesel engines started up and the big vessel moved away from the dock. Wherever she was going, she was on the way. Between the vibration of the engines and the rocking motion, Sarah's thoughts finally wound down and she drifted off to sleep.

She woke suddenly and found herself in her own bed, with Noah, and the relief that it had all been only a dream washed over her like a wave fifty feet high. She rolled over and wrapped her arms around him, and he turned his face toward her.

It wasn't Noah! The man she had wrapped her arms around was Lom, and he was laughing as he saw her pulling back. "Where is he?" she screamed at the thin old man, but he only laughed harder.

She tried to get up out of bed, but the sheets and blankets were tangling around her, pulling her back down, and then they were wrapping themselves around her face so that it was hard to breathe...

Buy Black Sheep now:
davidarcherbooks.com/black-sheep

Be the first to receive Noah Wolf updates. Sign up here:
davidarcherbooks.com/noah-updates

ALSO BY DAVID ARCHER

Not all books have been made into paperbacks yet, but I'm working on getting them all formatted and available as soon as possible.
Up to date paperbacks can be found on my website:
davidarcherbooks.com/pb

ALEX MASON THRILLERS
Odin (Book 1)
Ice Cold Spy (Book 2)
Mason's Law (Book 3)
Assets and Liabilities (Book 4)

NOAH WOLF THRILLERS
Code Name Camelot (Book 1)
Lone Wolf (Book 2)
In Sheep's Clothing (Book 3)
Hit for Hire (Book 4)
The Wolf's Bite (Book 5)
Black Sheep (Book 6)
Balance of Power (Book 7)
Time to Hunt (Book 8)
Red Square (Book 9)
Highest Order (Book 10)
Edge of Anarchy (Book 11)
Unknown Evil (Book 12)
Black Harvest (Book 13)
World Order (Book 14)

Caged Animal (Book 15)
Deep Allegiance (Book 16)
Pack Leader (Book 17)
High Treason (Book 18)
A Wolf Among Men (Book 19)
Rogue Intelligence (Book 20)

SAM PRICHARD MYSTERIES
The Grave Man (Book 1)
Death Sung Softly (Book 2)
Love and War (Book 3)
Framed (Book 4)
The Kill List (Book 5)
Drifter: Part One (Book 6)
Drifter: Part Two (Book 7)
Drifter: Part Three (Book 8)
The Last Song (Book 9)
Ghost (Book 10)
Hidden Agenda (Book 11)

SAM AND INDIE MYSTERIES
Aces and Eights (Book 1)
Fact or Fiction (Book 2)
Close to Home (Book 3)
Brave New World (Book 4)
Innocent Conspiracy (Book 5)
Unfinished Business (Book 6)
Live Bait (Book 7)
Alter Ego (Book 8)
More Than It Seems (Book 9)
Moving On (Book 10)
Worst Nightmare (Book 11)
Chasing Ghosts (Book 12)

CHANCE REDDICK THRILLERS

Made in United States
North Haven, CT
14 April 2023

35444247R00137